THE SECRET JUROR

BY

ROBIN BRANDE

THE SECRET JUROR
A Winnie Parsons Mystery
By Robin Brande

Published by Ryer Publishing
www.ryerpublishing.com
© 2025 Robin Brande
www.robinbrande.com
All rights reserved.
Art by talexstock and westode/Canva
Ebook ISBN: 978-1-952383-50-2
Print ISBN: 978-1-952383-51-9
Hardback ISBN: 978-1-952383-65-6

ALSO BY ROBIN BRANDE

<u>Winnie Parsons Mysteries</u>

A Mind for Mysteries (Collection)

The Genius Track

A Man of Appetites

A Drop of Sweat

The Long Gray Hook

The Slip of a Rib

The Cabin Ghost

The Secret Juror

The Truth Chamber

<u>Dove Season Universe</u>

Dove Season

Finder

Seeker

Believer

Maker

Explorer

<u>Self-Help</u>

What If You're Doing It Right?

What If You're Doing It Right? For Teens

THE SECRET JUROR

"There's something wrong with my judge."

Winnie served her niece Rose another thumbprint cookie. The Hershey Kiss in the middle of it had melted perfectly, just at its base, giving Rose the immediate chocolate and sugar infusion she needed after a stressful day in court.

Winnie hadn't expected to see her niece until at least the weekend, when maybe Rose could unwind.

She was wound-up now, still wearing her stylish navy blue suit and starched white blouse—less starched at the end of the day—but had already kicked off her navy pumps the moment she walked through the sanctuary of Winnie's door.

"Thank you," Rose said with a sigh as she bit into her third cookie. "I might need these in a first aid kit."

Rose's cheeks were flushed, bringing out the red of her strawberry blonde hair. Winnie recognized her look of frustration tinged with anger. Rose was a pro at controlling herself in court, but Winnie knew she needed the outlet of venting after particularly challenging days.

The outlet and the replenishing sugar Winnie always kept on hand. Rose was forty, with the hardy constitution of Winnie and her late brother, Rose's father. All of them had a sweet tooth, and Winnie felt no need to suffer by ignoring it.

She brought Rose a glass of water, set it on the coffee table between them, then nestled on the couch between her yellow Lab, Clover, and the Cavalier King Charles Spaniel she had recently adopted, a darling soul with the regal name of King Arthur.

King Arthur groaned and snuggled in closer. The late February days were starting to warm into the 70s—winter truly was the best time of year in Tucson—but the nights were still cold enough that the dogs sought out Winnie's warmth. She reached for the fleece blanket in the basket next to the couch and spread it over both dogs and herself. She had already tucked Rose into a blanket of her own. Winnie's first instinct was always to make everyone cozy.

At last Rose was replenished enough to slouch back in the chair and close her eyes for a moment. The flush on her cheeks had faded.

"All right," Rose said, sitting up straight and alert again. "Tell me what you think."

Judge William McCracken was one of those grizzled old judges who had probably stayed on the bench too long. There was an expiration date, Rose explained, for mental sharpness and judicial temperament. Judge McCracken was past his prime on both.

"I've appeared in front of him dozens of times over the years," Rose said. "I'm used to him. He can be a bear. It takes a certain touch. You need to be forceful but not aggressive. He doesn't mind you standing your ground, but he'll take your head off if he thinks you're arguing too much. He says he hates the noise."

Winnie always loved hearing Rose's stories from court. It was an exotic profession, as far as Winnie was concerned, and completely outside her own experiences as a former psychology professor. Rose's stories were like watching a courtroom drama on TV. Winnie grabbed another cookie for herself and readjusted her blanket.

"He lost his wife about a year ago," Rose said. "So … factor that in. Maybe."

Winnie nodded. She had lost her own beloved three years ago to cancer. Joe was still in her heart and mind every day. Maybe it was the same for Judge McCracken with his wife.

"But still," Rose said firmly. "There's a limit."

A week ago, during a hearing on Rose's and her

opposing counsel's pre-trial motions, Judge McCracken suddenly shouted at them both, "You're a couple of morons! Shut up!" He motioned angrily to his bailiff. "Get them out of here!"

Then he stood up and stormed out of the courtroom, leaving Rose, her opponent Alan Beasley, and Felicia, the judge's bailiff of many years, standing in stunned silence.

None of them understood what had happened.

"We went over it," Rose said. "We had the court reporter read back the last several lines of whatever we'd been arguing. It was all normal. Just the usual legal maneuvers. Nothing that should have set him off."

"Strange," Winnie said.

"That wasn't the end of it," Rose said. "By the time I got back to my office, there was an electronic ruling from the judge finding both Beasley and me in contempt of court. Fine of *fifteen hundred dollars* each. It was absolutely nuts. I've never had anything like that happen. Beasley either."

"What do you think that was about?" Winnie asked.

"Hold on," Rose said. "It gets weirder."

The trial was still scheduled to begin a week later. "Tomorrow," Rose said. "A jury trial, which means we're all supposed to be in place by eight-thirty, ready for the potential jurors to be brought in before nine. But Judge McCracken called Beasley and me into a special surprise hearing this afternoon and ordered us both to prepare a full extra brief on all the law we've already argued about for the last year in this case. It's like getting a snap assignment the night before a final exam. No judge would do that. I don't understand what this is about. It's like he's punishing us—again."

"Can you do it in time?" Winnie asked.

"I already did," Rose said. "It isn't pretty, but it's finished. I had my paralegal already file it. But I just wanted to talk to you before I headed home. See what you think about any of this."

Winnie's only experience with judges and court cases were from the times she had been called for jury duty over the years. She remembered having to arrive at the courthouse by 7:30 AM to fill out paperwork and watch an instructional video. Then the larger group received their assignments of which courtrooms they would go to. By 9:00 AM the jurors were usually hyped up on the free coffee and jittery from nerves anyway, and then the real tension of the morning began when they had to sit in a courtroom and listen to a real live judge call their names and ask them questions. It wasn't like watching it on television. It was both boring and nerve-racking.

Winnie had never yet been picked as a juror. The few times she came close, she fell back on her reliable and easiest to explain excuse.

"I'm a psychology professor," she'd tell the judge and the attorneys. "I'm sorry, but it's impossible for me to be impartial. I already have an opinion, just based on what I've already seen."

She knew that people were generally self-conscious being in the presence of psychologists and psychiatrists. People had told her so many times over the years. "I feel like you're always analyzing me."

"I am," Winnie would admit. "I can't help it."

But it was more than that. People seemed to assume psychology professionals had an almost mystical ability to see past flesh right into the heart and mind of a person.

Dr. Winifred Parsons's training in psychology didn't give her that.

But her gift as a clairvoyant did.

She really did know within moments of seeing the parties to a lawsuit which one of them was right and which had been wronged. She knew just from looking at the defendant in a criminal trial whether that person was guilty—of that or of other crimes.

It came to her in flashes of images and sounds and words.

Snatches of conversation. Mini-movies of scenes that told her the truth.

She knew it was the brother of the accused, a clean-cut young man sitting in the courtroom who seemed to be there to lend his brother support, who was actually the one guilty of burning down their parents' home.

She knew it was the secretary of a stockbroker sued

for fraud and embezzlement who had actually funneled the funds to herself and made it look like her boss was guilty.

Winnie did what she could after every visit to the courthouse to see that justice was actually done. Once Rose became a lawyer, sometimes she could help Winnie get the information to the right people. But before then Winnie had to rely on anonymous phone calls to law enforcement and anonymous notes slipped into law office mail slots laying out the truth of what had happened.

It was easier in the days before everyone had security cameras and caller ID. But Winnie still did her best.

What she really preferred was not to see that notice in her mail that she had been summoned to jury duty again. Going to court was low on her list of life's enjoyments.

Yet Winnie found herself saying to Rose now, "Would you like me to come tomorrow? See what I can see?"

"Oh, Aunt Winnie—would you?" Rose released the knot she'd made of her hands. Her face relaxed for the first time since she'd arrived.

"Let's eat something real," Winnie said, disturbing the cozy pile of blanket and dogs. "I need to know more about this."

2

____

It had been hard for Winnie in the beginning to cook delicious food for herself. What was the point? Joe was the one she loved to cook for.

It took months after he died for Winnie to rouse herself to make anything but toast and reheated cans of soup. She had no appetite. Food held no charm.

But the body wanted to live. Bodies want comfort. They want smells and tastes that delight their senses. They want sustenance, protein, breads, vegetables.

As the temperatures cooled that first autumn of widowhood, Winnie found she missed the stews she used to make. She missed baking fresh bread from her own sourdough starter.

She missed baking cookies. Even if Joe wasn't here anymore to savor her chocolate chip or peanut butter cookies, or to enjoy a slice of sour cream coffee cake fresh out of the oven—Winnie was still here. And Rose and her husband Matthew and their daughter Annabelle. And Rose's brother Danny and his wife and children. Winnie could cook for all of them. That was how she began. That was how she climbed out of the dark well where she'd been living.

She scheduled regular weekly dinners so she had a reason to try new recipes again. She found purpose in feeding her small circle of family.

And now her house smelled of cooking and baking all the time. Even when she wasn't expecting anyone else, she cooked for herself. She knew she had to. She had to live forward.

"What are these?" Rose asked. "I don't think I've ever seen them."

"Mushroom pot pie with drop biscuits for lids." It made for a neat little package. Winnie served them each two. No need to scrimp.

They sat at the kitchen table and ate in quiet for a few minutes. Winnie needed the silence as much as Rose did. Both of their minds were busy.

As she forked into the second biscuit, Winnie asked, "Does he seem ill?"

"No," Rose answered with her mouth full. "If you mean has he suddenly lost a bunch of weight or looks unsteady. He's normal as far as I can tell."

"What does Alan Beasley think?"

Rose gave a wry smile. "Well, he's stopped complaining that the judge keeps ruling in my favor. Sanctioning us both seemed to cure that."

"Has he ruled in your favor? Unusually?" Winnie asked.

"He agrees with a lot of my arguments," Rose said. "But it's because I'm actually right. Beasley's client is a slimebag. He cheated my people out of half a million dollars. The case law is on our side. Beasley should have settled this case long ago. But his guy still thinks he talk his way out of things."

"Can he?" Winnie asked. "Some people seem to be very slick at that."

"I don't know, you'll see what you think," Rose said as she scraped up the last of the mushroom and thyme-flavored cream sauce on her plate. "I think the jury's going to hate him."

3

———————

Winnie and the dogs had their morning routine. Even though he'd only been with them for a few weeks, King Arthur had learned it already.

Winnie awoke between 4:30 and 5:00. She never set an alarm. Those days were over.

She remembered reading some philosopher once who said that humans were the only creatures who believed that by breaking time into smaller units, they could actually make more of it.

Winnie wanted to feel each day stretching out in front of her, without chopping it into bits of having to be somewhere by this time or that.

But today she would accept the chopping, to help Rose. They agreed to meet at the courthouse at 8:00.

That was still a few hours away. For now, Winnie had the predawn darkness to herself.

The dogs were still asleep on top of her flannel bedspread, warmed by the electric blanket underneath. Winnie slipped out of bed and padded in socked feet into the kitchen to start her coffee brewing. Back in the bedroom she added a fleece top over her nightgown so she could sit up in bed and not feel chilled. She brushed her teeth and splashed cold water onto her face. By then the coffee was ready.

Winnie poured herself a mug of it and sprinkled cinnamon on top. She loved the smell of dark roast and spice to begin her day.

She brought the mug back with her into the bedroom and set it on the bedside table. Then she grabbed her notebook and a pen and slipped back between the covers without disturbing Clover, who was in the midst of a running dream. The Labrador puffed out muffled barks from her dream-inflated cheeks and moved all four paws as if she were chasing something. She probably was.

King Arthur softly snored. Winnie covered him with the extra fleece blanket she kept nearby just for him. King Arthur shivered more during the night than thick-coated Clover. Winnie had never had a small dog before. She had never had any dog until Clover. So dressing a small dog in little sweaters and jackets for winter walks was a new experience. But she was happy to take care of the dog with the kind of pampering she knew his former owner used to lavish on him.

Why even have animals if you couldn't spoil them?

Once everyone seemed settled and warm, Winnie turned out the bedside lamp and sat in the dark sipping her hot coffee. She breathed in the scent of the cinnamon. She deserved pampering, too.

Now she opened up her mind and let it wander.

Over the years Winnie found that people misunderstood the abilities of a clairvoyant. She wasn't all-knowing, all-seeing. She didn't know everything there was to know at any moment all across the world.

A talent like that would burn out a mind in short order. No one could hold that level of openness and focus for more than a few minutes.

It would be like hearing every single song and symphony and opera and instrumental ever written in the history of mankind—and hearing them all at the same time—then asking the mind to single out just four important notes to focus on in the midst of the chaos of sound. It just wasn't possible. A mind didn't work that way.

Instead, Winnie had learned to use her clairvoyance to focus her mind on seeing, hearing, and knowing the things she wanted to explore.

She thought about it as stepping into a vast warehouse and shining her flashlight in certain areas, rather than flipping on the overhead lights and flooding her mind with overstimulation. If every shred of information came pouring into her mind at once, she'd have no way of organizing it all to make sense of it. This way she could take it in with some kind of order, and use both the analytical and clairvoyant parts of her mind to sort out the pieces together.

Winnie was ready to explore the endless warehouse of information now.

Last night Rose had shown her several photographs of Judge William McCracken posted on the internet. There were photos from his days as a litigator a few decades ago, and more recent images of him at his current age, which the internet put at 69. Just a year older than Winnie.

He looked very stern in his judicial photo.

"Judges don't really smile for their pictures," Rose said. "They all want to be taken seriously."

Judge McCracken was enough of a local public figure that the news a year ago noted the passing of his wife.

Helen McCracken died peacefully at home, it said, at the age of 66. Young by Winnie's standards. Helen had recently retired from her position as a Language Arts teacher at Canyon Road Junior High. There was a picture of William and Helen McCracken that might have been taken ten years ago on what looked like a cruise ship. They looked happy enough.

"I don't suppose you ever met her," Winnie asked Rose.

"No. We had no reason to socialize."

Now in the darkness of her bedroom, cozy beneath her blankets, a mug of hot coffee warming her hands, Winnie closed her eyes and let her mind begin its search for whatever it might want to show her about Helen McCracken. Like Rose said, her death might mean nothing to Judge McCracken's current behavior, but only one year after the death of a spouse was barely any time at all. If he was anything like Winnie had been, he was still in a fog of disbelief. How could his wife really be gone?

Winnie heard a gentle laugh. It made her smile. She saw no images, but the laugh was something. Winnie took another sip of coffee and kept her eyes closed and waited for more.

"Bill..."

Then ... silence for a moment, then...

"Helen? ... Helen! HELEN!"

Winnie's eyes sprang open.

Her skin felt cold.

A thin sheen of sweat moistened her face.

Winnie gave a cough. Then a harder cough that spilled coffee from her mug onto her sheet.

She set down the coffee and sat up straighter in bed and tried to hold the image she had just seen.

It was not a slowly advancing death like the one Joe had gone through.

Helen McCracken died suddenly. Not "peacefully at home"—although maybe that was a matter of interpretation.

She was at home, sitting in her chair, reading a book. She must have laughed at something she read. Winnie heard it.

Judge McCracken sat in his own chair watching the news on TV.

"Bill..."

"Hm?" He glanced over. Just in time to see his wife slump in her chair. Her book slipped from her hands and fell to the floor.

"Helen?" Then realizing something had happened. He rushed to her. Called to her. Shouted her name.

But in that brief space of time, Helen McCracken was gone.

Winnie watched the judge maneuver her onto the floor and begin CPR. He seemed to remember the steps and paused to frantically call 911. He sputtered out his address and resumed compressions on Helen's chest.

The scene faded. Winnie's mind must have known it had shown her enough. Tears pricked Winnie's eyes. The look on William McCracken's face had been one of shock and agony. Winnie hated to see anyone's pain.

She turned on her light. Then she began writing in her notebook quickly, to record as much as she could capture of even the smallest of details: what they both were wearing. What time of day it seemed based on the light coming through the windows. What furniture was in their living room. Any detail she had noticed.

This wasn't so she could read it later or show it to anyone. She didn't need to prove what she had seen— even to herself.

But over the years Winnie had discovered that by writing the details down, her mind seemed encouraged to feed her even more. Images and sounds sharpened. Information became clearer. Colors, smells, textures: the more she could signal to her clairvoyant mind that she was paying attention, the more details streamed into her perception.

She saw herself in partnership ... with herself. There was the Winnie who saw and knew, and the Winnie outside herself, viewing it and listening and learning as much as she could.

After writing continuously for four pages, recording everything she observed about Helen McCracken's death, Winnie finally stopped. Her face still felt clammy. Her fingers were stiff and cold. The fleece top she had put on over her flannel nightgown wasn't enough to keep her warm.

Winnie turned up the heat on her electric blanket and slid down between her covers. She felt very, very sorry for William McCracken. No one wanted to go through what he did.

But there was no denying what happened. Just as Winnie had to remind herself every day for months after Joe died. She didn't want it ... but that didn't matter. Joe was gone and no amount of wishing would change that truth.

All she could do was live forward. All she could do was take the next step and the next. Then wake up another day and do it again.

She wondered if Judge McCracken had discovered that yet for himself.

4

By 7:15 AM the dogs were next door with Winnie's neighbor, Dawn, who had a long-haired Dachshund named Sporty who was not. He preferred lying in the sun and under fluffy blankets all day while Dawn worked remotely managing airline reservations. Winnie brought over Clover's and King Arthur's dog beds, but it was just as likely they would curl up on the couch in Dawn's office if Sporty chose to make some room.

At 8:00 AM, Winnie stood outside the Superior Court building dressed in gray drawstring velour pants, quilted gray boots, and a navy blue sweater. She wore a dark gray thigh-length winter coat and a gray fleece hat over her short wavy white-blonde hair. Her wire-rim glasses looked standard for an old lady.

She was utterly forgettable, which was exactly the

point. Just another senior citizen, probably either some lawyer's client or maybe a juror. No one of any importance. Look away.

She and Rose had decided the night before not to appear as if they were together. Although the courtroom was open to the public, Judge McCracken might not like it if one of the lawyers in the case decided to bring along family, as if this were a school performance and not a serious professional matter. As if Rose might turn around and wave to her aunt in the middle of questioning a witness.

Absurd, but they both agreed that it was better to play it safe. The judge was too hard to predict.

Rose told Winnie to wait for her outside the court building so she could at least show her the way. No need to wander the halls of the courthouse looking for the right floor and the right room.

From the outside, the Superior Court looked like any other eight-floor office building. No character at all. Unlike the historic Justice Court building to the left of it, with its washed-out pink stucco exterior and distinctive turquoise dome on top. Winnie could imagine it passing for an old mission church if the people going in and out wore long monkish robes instead of suits.

The air was still crisp, especially in the shade near the entrance. Winnie could see her breath. She found a spot to wait in the sunshine so she could feel its warmth on her hands and face. A large stone fountain burbled nearby. She wondered if anyone sat on the edges and dipped their feet in it during the roasting summers. The landscaping this time of year was less than inspiring, with the planters in front of the courthouse filled with just cacti and gravel.

Winnie caught sight of Rose now hurrying from the sidewalk up the set of wide concrete steps. Seeing her niece here in her element, looking so smart and polished and confident, Winnie felt a surge of love and pride. Rose looked in command of her world. She wore a dark gray pin-striped suit, an ivory silk blouse, black pumps, and an overcoat the same charcoal gray as Winnie's, but much more stylish and tailored.

Rose saw her and gave her a quick smile. Then she kept on walking past her to the entrance and went in through the heavy wooden doors.

Winnie followed her lead. She placed her gray quilted purse—another old lady prop she never used in real life—behind Rose's briefcase on the conveyor belt that fed items through the scanning machine. The female security guard asked Winnie if she had a pacemaker—she didn't—then motioned Winnie through the metal detector.

The first floor was a hive of industry, with well-dressed people carrying paperwork and stacks of files to and from various rooms. It was obvious who knew their way around and who didn't. Winnie recognized the lost looks of ordinary citizens there for jury duty, or to find where to get their marriage licenses, or needing help navigating some aspect of the legal system here in a place that could seem imposing and bewildering.

Even though Winnie had been in the courthouse before, she appreciated being able to follow Rose, who clearly knew every nook of this place. The two of them retrieved their belongings from the security station and headed straight for the pair of elevators on the first floor.

Where Winnie's cover was blown.

"Well you just made my morning."

Winnie turned at the sound of his voice, already smiling at the face she knew she would see.

"Came to see the wreckage?" Rose muttered to one of her closest friends from law school.

Troy Vargas, tall, black, and movie-star handsome in his own tailored suit, ignored her for a moment while he bent down and gave Winnie a hug.

"Aunt Win, any day that starts with seeing you has to be a winner. And no," he told Rose, "I'm not just a looky-loo." Troy angled closer and said discreetly, "I have a trial in front of McCracken in two weeks. Need to see for myself what's coming."

"Nothing good," Rose said.

"Yeah, I heard. Fifteen hundred bucks. Pricey."

Rose gave him a warning look as two men joined them at the elevators.

"Alan," Troy said. Winnie wondered if this was Rose's

opponent, Alan Beasley. He was only slightly shorter than Troy, but his slouch took away another inch or two. He was too thin for his head, but otherwise not unpleasant looking. He gave Troy a vacant nod and went back to reading something on his phone.

Winnie had to take a step back from the man standing next to Beasley. He reeked. He was in his fifties, with thick brown hair he must have paid a lot to have dyed such a natural color, and he wore an expensive suit and shined leather shoes.

Surrounding him was a cloud of dark gray, as dark as Rose's charcoal coat. Acid-green puffs of air continuously burped from the areas around his chest and throat. Winnie realized this was what she was smelling. No one else in the vicinity seemed to notice his stench. As sometimes happened, she didn't just see the man's aura, she could smell it: a rancid blend of musky cologne, stale breath, and a week's worth of old sweat.

Winnie covered her nose. Rose caught the gesture and glanced at Beasley's client, the man she had described to Winnie as a slimeball. Then even though Rose pretended to concentrate on the floor numbers displayed above the elevators, Winnie saw her small smile of triumph. Winnie had agreed with her assessment.

The elevator on the left dinged. As Rose and others crowded on, Winnie tugged Troy aside. "Let's take the next one," she whispered. "I'm supposed to be incognito."

What she really wanted to avoid was being trapped in a closed elevator with that stench. But she didn't tell that to Troy Vargas. He was unaware of Winnie's clairvoyant capabilities. He was smart enough to know she was sensitive and even exceptionally intuitive, but Winnie had never yet felt the need to tell him the whole truth.

"Not a bad idea," Troy said. "I'm half-afraid to go in there myself."

"So you agree, there's something strange about Judge McCracken now?"

"Not really," Troy said. "Just have to listen to the rumors."

Winnie wasn't surprised that Troy might know things Rose didn't. Ever since they were in law school, he always seemed to have the inside track on the various personalities all around them.

Winnie and Joe lived close to the University of Arizona law school, so Rose and Troy and a few other classmates in their study group made a habit of coming over a few nights a week for Winnie's home-cooked meals and a comfortable place to study away from the law library.

After the meal Joe usually retreated to his study to watch sports or news on TV, but Winnie liked to hang around the kitchen, cleaning or puttering or baking, so she could listen to Rose and her friends in the adjoining living room.

She loved to hear them buoy each other up—*"Are you kidding? No one could have gotten that one"*—and challenge each other, and argue about the cases in their textbooks and whether justice had been done.

And yes, gossip.

Troy Vargas was the master of it.

He knew which professors were "seeing each other," as he put delicately when Winnie was around. He knew which students had been caught cheating. Who got the premium offers for internships. Who was dropping out because the whole thing was too much for them. Troy always had a few new stories every night. Even though Winnie didn't know any of the players, she was still fascinated by the intrigue.

Troy didn't treat it like gossip, it was useful information. The more they knew, the better. It helped them all navigate the system.

Aside from her niece, Troy had always been Winnie's favorite in the group. He was a kind young man with a dry wit and insights into human nature that often surprised Winnie—even though as a psychology professor, she was supposed to be the expert.

She waited to find out more about Troy's current inside information while they rode an elevator full of what looked like more lawyers and various court personnel. Most of them seemed to know Troy.

"Keeping you busy?" one of the lawyers asked him.

"You know it," Troy said, and Winnie wondered how many times they all had conversations just like that.

When Winnie taught at the university, the canned dialogue from some of the professors was usually, "Is the semester over yet?" The real jokers liked to say it the first week of classes.

The two of them got out on the sixth floor. A wide hallway separated sets of imposing wooden doors leading to individual courtrooms. Troy found a quiet spot where they could continue their conversation outside the bustle of the morning's legal activities.

"McCracken's almost seventy," Troy continued as if they'd never been interrupted. "Birthday's in a month and a half." He paused while a group of jurors passed in front of them, following their minder into one of the courtrooms. "Mandatory retirement," he went on. "Heard he tried to fight it. But good luck. Seventy is seventy. You're out."

"So you think he's just lashing out?" Winnie asked. "Acting erratically because he's angry?"

"Or losing it," Troy said. "Man can be tightly wound."

Troy watched another set of citizens being led to another courtroom. "That's McCracken's," he said. "We'd better get in there. If you want to blend, go in with them."

Winnie followed his advice. She trailed behind the group of twenty or so potential jurors and pretended she belonged.

The courtroom looked like so many of the ones Winnie saw on TV: low blue-gray carpeting, dark wood benches, black laminate tables at the front of the room where the lawyers sat with their clients. The judge's desk, currently unoccupied, stood on a raised platform at the center of the furthest wall.

Rose and her two clients sat at the table on the right, closest to the empty jury box. Alan Beasley and his rancid-smelling client sat at the table on the left.

The lawyers and their clients all stood up and faced the jurors as they filed into the room. Winnie wondered if it was just a quaint bit of manners left over from the old days, or a useful bit of strategy: Don't look like you're hiding. Be polite. Smile. Try to get the jury on your side from the start.

Winnie found a seat on one of the padded benches toward the back. It reminded her of a church pew, but newer. Troy sat next to her. Once all of the jurors settled in, the lawyers and their clients sat, too. Rose went back to conferring with her clients, Jennie and Mike Tudor, a modest-looking couple in their forties who Winnie could see were very nervous. Both of them had a hard time focusing on Rose. They glanced repeatedly at their opponent. Litigation was stressful.

But apparently not for the slimeball, Vic Barr. He looked relaxed and even bored, as if being sued and having to face a judge and jury were nothing to him. Maybe it had happened often enough, this was just routine. Winnie didn't know and couldn't sense the answer. She watched him sit with his arm draped over the empty chair to his left while his lawyer ignored him and made notes on a yellow legal pad.

Winnie could still see the puffs of acid green bursting out of the dark gray aura surrounding Barr. At least this far away she couldn't smell him.

Winnie switched her attention to focus on the overall room. She could feel the mood of the assembled group: a kind of tension—some of it excitement, some of it dread —while everyone waited for the show to begin.

Some of the potential jurors had gone back to reading their books or looking at their phones, but some sat staring at the lawyers and their clients, the only actors currently on the scene.

Winnie continued watching the slimeball. A puff of acid-green rose from the right side of his head and burst into an array of smaller pellets. It seemed impossible that the slimeball's lawyer hadn't smelled it, but he continued scribbling on his legal pad, oblivious.

"What do you think of Alan Beasley?" Winnie whispered to Troy.

"Lightweight. C-student. Rosie'll have no trouble."

"Did you go to school with him?"

"No," Troy said, "but you can always tell."

Winnie would have loved to hear more—including

how Troy came to rate his fellow attorneys and guess at their grades from back in law school—but just then the door at the far wall opened and the judge's bailiff came through, followed by two other women.

The bailiff was a sturdy-looking Hispanic woman in her early fifties with a lively orange and rose-colored aura. Winnie had a sense of her immediately: Reliable. Honorable. Loyal. And Winnie didn't need her clairvoyance to see that the woman was no nonsense.

The other two women, both a little younger than the bailiff, wore office attire and looked equally serious in their roles. The one with the long braid sat at the desk next to the bailiff, and the other sat at a modular desk and chair closer to the judge's raised platform. The court clerk and the court reporter, Winnie guessed.

"All rise," the bailiff called out as Judge McCracken entered through the same private door.

Winnie recognized him, of course, but not so much from the photographs she and Rose had looked at the night before. She had spent time with him this morning, reliving what had to be his most painful memory. She could still see the look of panic on his face as he rushed to his wife and frantically tried to revive her.

And now, a year later, she saw the lingering anguish on his face. Some might interpret his expression as surly or hostile, but all she saw was pain. What's more, she could see the many rips in his pale blue auric field. Judge McCracken's energy was leaking out all over.

He settled behind his desk—what Winnie knew was called the judge's bench—and spent a moment surveying his kingdom. Taking in the lawyers, the clients, and the citizens sitting in back.

His gaze passed over Winnie and landed on Troy.

"Mr. Vargas?" the judge asked sharply. "Are you lost?"

"No, your honor." Troy gave Winnie's wrist a squeeze and muttered, "Oh well. Tell Rosie I said good luck." He stood and gave the judge a short, respectful nod, and quietly exited the courtroom.

Winnie was sorry to see him go, but she understood why Troy didn't fight it. He had his own upcoming trial to think of. It was better to stay on the judge's good side, if that was possible.

Winnie and Rose exchanged a quick glance. Rose's clients looked more nervous than ever.

Whereas the slimeball looked completely at ease, acid-green puffs belching off his fetid aura.

Winnie hoped Rose could wipe that cocky smirk off the man's face.

5

If Winnie were a concert pianist, she often thought, she would think nothing of practicing her scales every day. They would keep her fingers nimble. They would solidify her relationship with her instrument.

Her psi ability was no different: a gift, a talent—one she could strengthen and improve with daily practice.

She knew other clairvoyants who simply relied on their natural abilities. There was nothing wrong with that.

But maybe it was like Troy Vargas said about Alan Beasley: C-student. A lightweight. That wasn't good enough for Winnie. Not because she wanted to compete with anyone, but just for her own internal satisfaction.

She always wanted to know more and learn more. It was why she enjoyed her decades as a professor. She learned something new every day, whether from her own research or from conversations with her colleagues, or from interactions with her bright and curious students.

And now, sitting in a room full of strangers, she knew it was a perfect opportunity to practice.

In her youth, before she learned how to deliberately turn down her perceptions of the people around her, Winnie avoided being in public places. Seeing so many auras, sensing so many different thoughts and feelings pouring off the strangers around her, Winnie would return home feeling absolutely spent. It took her hours to climb down from the sensory and mental overload.

But once she began studying how others in the psi community learned to moderate their focus, she was able to dial it down. Stop letting the images and sensations come flooding in. If she wanted to know something about someone she could always open up her perception again. But on a normal day she no longer felt the need to take to her bed and cut off all outside stimulation until the sensation of overload passed.

Winnie turned up her dials now. She wanted to know.

Sight. Sound. Inner knowing.

Rose and Beasley were in the process of picking their jury. It meant they were allowed to ask the potential jurors all sorts of personal questions to root out any bias.

Name, address, occupation. What bumper stickers are on your car? What magazines do you read? (One of the younger citizens, a bartender who looked like she was barely old enough to drink, snickered at that. As in *What's a magazine?* Apparently she and her friends only read their phones.)

The judge asked some of the questions himself: Has anyone here been involved in a lawsuit? Has anyone been accused of fraud?

Winnie watched people's body language change at the same time the colors and intensities of their auras did, too. She knew when the person was about to lie.

Only one person, a CPA dressed in a business suit, raised her hand to admit she had been sued. But Winnie saw two other people in the room who clearly withheld that information.

One was a middle-aged man dressed in khakis and a black sweater whose aura went from a pale lilac to a dark, angry purple. Winnie could feel the humiliation pumping through his veins, like a sudden rush of poison.

The other was a mousy-looking woman dressed in as much gray as Winnie was. She looked about Winnie's same age.

Even though the woman didn't raise her hand to admit she had been accused of fraud, Winnie saw her aura undergo an immediate and dramatic change. Whereas before the color of it had been a dull, neutral rust, now rings of bright yellow spun around her throat, and dots of black and shocking pink pockmarked the outline of her skull and continued down the length of her arms. There was nothing subtle about it: the woman in gray looked as if she had suddenly contracted a strange exotic disease. One that made her squirm in her chair as if her skin were on fire.

Winnie no longer questioned what she saw in people's auras. All of the colors meant something, and Winnie tried to learn from what she saw to create her own personal color chart. Another clairvoyant looking at the woman in gray might see completely different colors. It was as specific to each clairvoyant as their sense of taste and smell.

Winnie had not seen this particular combination of honeybee yellow and black and cartoon pink. She would add them to her catalog of auras later.

But first she needed to know what the colors meant. She needed to know what this woman had done.

As information streamed into her mind, Winnie sat back and watched it like a mini-movie playing just for her.

The woman in gray was maybe twenty years younger than she was now. Unlike her plain, old lady outfit today, she wore festive red sweatpants and a dark green sweatshirt with a bright red Christmas tree on the front. Winnie saw her kneeling on the tan carpeting inside someone's closet. Winnie could smell the musty clothes hanging above her.

She could hear people talking in a nearby room. The

woman heard them, too. She looked nervous. Skittish. But she went ahead with what she was doing.

She fished out a cardboard file box from the back of the closet and removed the lid. Inside Winnie saw a tightly-packed row of labeled file folders. The woman quickly fingered through them to find the one she wanted.

Winnie didn't see the label on the folder, but she saw the document inside. It was typewritten on heavy bond paper, with old-fashioned lettering on top. There were perhaps a dozen pages held together with a binder clip. Winnie felt as if she were peering over the woman's shoulder, rather than examining the document at her own leisure. But she managed to see the title of it before the woman removed the binder clip and hurriedly turned to another page:

Last Will and Testament.

About halfway through the document the woman found what she was looking for. Winnie watched as the woman in Christmas sweats removed two pages from the will.

There was a plain manila folder on the carpet near the woman's right knee. Winnie hadn't noticed it before. The woman took out two pieces of paper from it—pages that looked similar to the ones in the original will, right down to the handwritten initials in the designated space at the top of each page indicating that whoever the will was for had read those pages and approved them.

Peering over the woman's shoulder, Winnie couldn't get a good enough look at the pages to read what they now said. But she assumed the person's will now left money or property to the woman in the Christmas sweats, whereas maybe it didn't before. And maybe an heir named in the will wasn't anymore.

Someone laughed in the nearby room. The woman froze and listened. Winnie could feel her fear—and excitement. The woman's heart raced, she was definitely afraid, but Winnie could also feel her secret delight. As if the woman in the Christmas sweats were doing something she'd thought of doing for a long time, but never had the courage until now.

As soon as the conversation in the next room resumed, the woman quickly completed her task. She swapped out the pages of the will, straightened everything and clipped it all back together, then returned the document to its file folder. She slid the folder back into the box where it belonged, and added her own folder, now empty, further along toward the back. She refit the cardboard lid on top and pushed the box back against the closet wall.

The whole enterprise may have taken only a few minutes. The woman seemed very pleased with herself.

Not at all guilty that she had deliberately and fraudulently just altered someone's will.

As a last step, the woman folded up the two pages she had removed and stuffed them down the front of her red sweatpants. She pulled her Christmas tree sweatshirt lower to hide the awkward shape.

The scene faded. Winnie was back in the courtroom staring at the back of the mousy woman's head.

Not so mousy. Not so meek. A bold and outrageous thief.

The woman in question was looking down, as if trying to avoid anyone seeing her.

But Winnie saw her, saw her very clearly.

And yet there was nothing she could do about it.

Rose was busy. She had moved on to asking the potential jurors another set of questions. Winnie wasn't going to raise her hand and point to the woman in gray and say, "Do *not* pick her for your jury. She's a slimeball, too."

But then something else caught Winnie's attention. A change had come over the judge. Now instead of seeing only the various rips in William McCracken's pale blue auric field, for the first time Winnie saw the cause.

There were needles sticking out all over his body. Long thin blades the size of cooking skewers. Hundreds of them. Most of them were concentrated around his throat and his heart. Everywhere the needles pierced him, his aura had turned a dark and bloody red.

Judge McCracken looked exhausted. His shoulders sloped forward in his chair. He looked twenty years older than when he first walked into the courtroom. Winnie had no idea what might have happened in the last several minutes to bring about such a drastic change.

The judge didn't seem to be paying any attention to what was going on in his courtroom. Instead he wrote on a pad of paper in front of him. Short, repetitive movements with his pen that made Winnie think he was drawing, rather than writing.

Then suddenly, maybe through some force of will, Judge McCracken came back to himself. Back to the courtroom.

And he wasn't happy about it.

"That's enough!" he blurted out, interrupting Rose in the middle of a question. "Get on with it and pick your jury. These people have been here long enough. You have fifteen minutes," he ordered Rose and Beasley. "Everyone else, recess."

The judge didn't need to bang his gavel. His voice was harsh enough. He abruptly stood, catching his bailiff off guard. She managed to call out, "All rise," just in time for the judge to sweep past her through his private door. Winnie saw the bailiff exchange a worried look with the court clerk. Obviously this wasn't normal.

Winnie watched the court clerk and bailiff speak quietly to each other before exiting the courtroom through that same back door. Meanwhile the potential jurors wandered out of the courtroom, most of them probably in search of the restrooms.

Winnie needed a break, too, but first she had to speak to Rose. There was the matter of the mousy woman—Winnie had to make sure Rose didn't pick her for the jury—but more important, Winnie was now very concerned about the judge.

She had seen something. She had seen it all. And what Winnie saw was alarming.

Rose was deep in conversation with Alan Beasley as the two of them examined the list of jurors' names on both their computer tablets. If Rose was angry or embarrassed about how the judge had just spoken to her, she was an experienced enough trial lawyer not to show it. Only Winnie noticed the brief blaze of color on her pale cheeks.

Winnie pulled out her cell phone. Everyone had to turn theirs off while court was in session, but it must be all right now.

Rose's was probably still off, but Winnie still sent her a text message:

Not the old woman in gray sitting in front of me.

No, she needed to do better. What was the woman's

name? Winnie couldn't remember. It was no use trying to force it. Her mind had better ways to work.

Winnie closed her eyes for a moment and waited for the name to come.

As soon as she relaxed, it was like toast popping up in a toaster.

She erased the text and typed a new one:

Not Angela Whitmere. I'll explain later. The judge is in serious danger. I have to help him TODAY. See if you can get him to speak to me.

Winnie played the part of a chatty elder woman. "Oh, a text!" she said loudly enough for Rose to hear her. Rose glanced over. Winnie waggled her phone as if sharing this delight with a stranger.

Winnie assumed Rose understood to look at her own phone. With that work done, Winnie headed for the exit.

She wasn't sure how Rose would be able to manage arranging a meeting between Winnie and the judge today, but it had to happen. This was too important to wait. If Winnie could help the man at all, it had to be done as soon as possible.

Judge McCracken's life could depend on it.

6

It was something Winnie had learned over the years from studying and teaching human psychology: Even when we can't understand why people do what they do, we should assume there's a payoff. We should assume that in some way it is working for them, even if to outside eyes their behavior seems irrational or self-destructive.

A few years before she retired from the university, Winnie attended a conference where one of the speakers was a French psychologist named Dr. Berne.

His presentation still remained one of her favorites. Anyone who heard it would remember it. Dr. Berne gave examples of familiar behaviors, but also one that was more outrageous: Why does this man pick his nose at the office when co-workers sitting beside him are clearly disgusted? Why does this woman continue giving money to her boyfriend when she knows without a doubt he spends it on other women? Why does a son call his mother every night just to hear her criticize him and tell him he is a failure?

"Some might say these people suffer from poor self-esteem," Dr. Berne told the group. "Some might say the man who picks his nose is simply a pig."

But Dr. Berne compared the nature of their professions in psychology to having a sore in your mouth that you can't stop bothering with your tongue. Or finding a bruise on your arm and pressing your finger into it just to see if it hurts.

"We have to know," he said. "We are curious. We are investigators. We think we see the truth ... but are we correct? We will ask more questions. We will persevere. We will give these people our complete attention and not rush to tell them why they are wrong. We will not assume we are already so smart and have nothing left to learn."

Dr. Berne pretended to hold a notebook and write on it. "So you pick your nose. I see. You give your cheating boyfriend all your money. I see. You talk to your mother who is clearly a—" Dr. Berne offered a few French words that some people understood and others like Winnie simply guessed at, and that made all of them laugh. Dr. Berne pretended to write it down. "*Oui*. I see.

"What we must do," Dr. Berne told the audience, "is always search for *la raison sage*. The wise reason. It is there. What is the benefit? Where is the profit? We are professionals and must do better than simply saying, 'Ah, do not do that anymore. It is disgusting. It is pointless. It is painful.'

"So shall I tell you why the man picks his nose at work?"

Winnie and the rest of the audience replied as one, "Yes!"

"Because he is also the man who calls his mother every night so that she can complain and criticize and tell him he is a failure. He picks his nose because he loves his mother. If he were successful, well-liked, well-groomed, with a loving girlfriend or wife and several loving children, his mother would be abandoned. His mother who raised him by herself and who has cried at every stage of having to let him go: the first day of school. The first day of university. The day he moved out and became a man on his own. This is intolerable, and the man who picks his nose feels it here." Dr. Berne laid his hand on his heart. "He does not know it here." He pointed to his temple. "But perhaps you are the one to realize that the man is disgusting because he is full of love. And that, my friends, is the gift we can offer those who are suffering. People do what they do for a reason. How wonderful it is to be able to help them understand themselves."

Dr. Berne gave a gracious bow as Winnie and the rest of the audience rose to their feet. It was one of the few standing ovations Winnie recalled at any of the conferences she attended. Psychologists were not normally so enthusiastic, but the man's words and demeanor and spirit seemed to lift up everyone there.

People do what they do for a reason. They may not know it in their minds, but they know it in their hearts. They know it in their souls.

Winnie checked her watch. She still had five minutes left of their break. Enough time to find a quiet place down the hall from the restrooms where she could replay certain images in her mind.

She slowed the pictures down, like a sporting event's play-by-play, so she could study the images more clearly: the terrible clustering of needles all over Judge McCracken's body. The way they penetrated his aura and left dark and bloody wounds at their tips.

But then.

"That's enough! Get on with it and pick your jury!"

That burst of hostility, that rudeness, was enough to make all of the needles retract. In a flash, the dark red wounds were gone, and the judge's aura was back to its original pale blue outline.

Although now there were clearly more tears in it than before, and some were wider than Winnie remembered from earlier this morning. She realized with alarm that he was leaking: leaking emotion, leaking energy, leaking his fundamental life's vitality.

Winnie had seen leaking like that become a flood. She watched it with her husband, Joe, the last few weeks of his life. The vitality drained out of him right before her eyes. One day he was still himself, the next day he wasn't.

Not long after, he faded into a coma. The last time Winnie spoke to him it was in a vision, his vitality restored. But the physical Joe was gone.

And now Judge McCracken was in danger of the same downward drain. Maybe not right away, but soon. Maybe even before his seventieth birthday. Troy said it was a month and a half away.

A birthday that would force Judge McCracken out of a job that might be keeping him alive for now. From what Winnie had seen, the judge still had enough innate will to survive that a kind of aggression took over, maybe to forcibly snap him back to life. Like someone with sleep apnea waking himself up when his brain signaled it was not getting enough oxygen.

La raison sage. The wise reason. People did what they did for a reason. Whether they understood themselves or not.

The judge had become aggressive because it was the only way to make the needles disappear. He was doing it to keep his life from draining away. But the needles were still there. Still piercing him and leaving open wounds.

Winnie wasn't sure how she could help him, but she knew she had to try.

7

"All rise."

This time when Judge McCracken passed his bailiff he gave her a nod of acknowledgment. Maybe they had spoken in the privacy of his chambers. Maybe they were friends enough that Felicia the bailiff could ask him if he was feeling all right, or could cautiously mention he was a little over the top before.

Winnie had no idea how the hierarchy of courtrooms worked. Were judges approachable? They were human beneath their black robes, but maybe they were conscious of never appearing vulnerable, even to the staff around them.

With everyone seated again, the judge read off the juror list that Rose and Beasley had provided. Winnie was glad to hear that the will-fraudster's name was not on the list.

"Ladies and gentlemen," the judge told the remaining people, "thank you for your time today. The justice system depends on people like you. We appreciate your service."

Winnie studied the judge's aura. It seemed a slightly darker shade of blue now. Overall he looked a little healthier. The rips in his aura were not leaking as much as fifteen minutes ago.

Maybe just that short rest had been enough to restore some of his equilibrium.

With the selected jury now seated in their desig-nated chairs at the front of the room, Winnie realized she was suddenly the only citizen still sitting out in the gallery.

Judge McCracken noticed that, too.

"Ma'am? You're excused. Thank you."

"Oh, I..." Winnie looked to Rose for guidance. They hadn't discussed this scenario. Rose stood up and looked ready to give some explanation—probably to confess that Winnie was with her—but Winnie bowled on. She stood to address the judge. "My friend isn't picking me up until this afternoon. She's not always easy to reach. Would it be all right if I stayed in here? Your honor?"

If Winnie read the man right, he would not throw some old lady out on the courthouse steps—in the cold of winter, at that—to wait for the next several hours for her ride. And Rose had said that courtrooms were technically open to the public.

And yet the judge had already effectively thrown out Troy Vargas, who had just as much right to be there. Winnie wasn't sure what the judge would say.

He said nothing. He gave her a somewhat begrudging nod, Winnie sat down, and she saw the color of his aura start to fade once again. Whatever burst of hardiness Judge McCracken had a few moments ago was gone. Winnie hated to think she had been the cause of this latest depletion. For now, all she could do was observe.

It was now close to 11:00. Jury selection had taken about two hours. If it were up to Winnie, she might have sent everyone out on an early lunch, but it was not up to her. Judge McCracken said the attorney for the plaintiffs would now present her opening statement.

Rose looked relaxed and confident as she stepped out from behind her table and faced the jury.

"Ladies and gentleman, your honor," she gave a nod to the judge, "I represent Mike and Jennie Tudor. I don't mind telling you they have been sweethearts since high school. They were those kinds of kids you see in movies who meet when they answer a bulletin on the cafeteria board to come for tryouts to join a band. Thirty years and two daughters later, they're still together."

Despite her nervousness, Jennie Tudor smiled. Mike reached over and held her hand.

Winnie could see that a few women on the jury and surprisingly, the gruff-looking contractor with the big bushy beard, all had the same reaction she did: they smiled at the sweetness of Rose's story.

Rose knew how to present her case.

"The music business is a tough one," Rose went on. "Very, very few musicians ever make a career of it. But Jennie and Mike have been doing just that, at least locally, for the past many years. They play at all the various resorts around Tucson. They perform at weddings and reunions and corporate events. They usually work at least five nights a week, year round. Sometimes it's just the two of them—they're both singers, and Jennie plays the keyboard, Mike plays guitar—and sometimes they perform with other musicians. All in all, Jennie and Mike have done what they set out to do back in their freshman year of high school. They've created for themselves a happy and successful life."

Rose gestured toward the slimeball. "But then they met the defendant, Victor Barr."

Just from having her attention drawn to him again, Winnie caught another strong whiff of him, even from several rows back. This time she smelled unwashed body and greasy hair and a blast of rancid, rotting garbage. Winnie discreetly covered her nose with her hand. If Rose noticed, she didn't let it distract her.

"What we will show you," Rose told the jury, "is how

the defendant systematically defrauded Jennie and Mike not only of their current livelihood, but of any future they have in the music business."

Winnie already knew the story. Rose had told her all of it the night before. How Vic Barr tricked Jennie and Mike Tudor into signing various agreements that robbed them of control over their own music.

Jennie Tudor wrote her own songs. Beautiful, lyrical, heart-felt songs people loved to hear over and over. Jennie and Mike poured their own money into making three albums that they sold in resort gift shops and online with several streaming services. Jennie and Mike hadn't made a fortune with any of it so far, but it gave them a nice steady cash stream to supplement what they made from their regular live performances.

Rose played one of Jennie's songs for Winnie last night, and it almost made Winnie cry. It was like a dart to the heart, straight in, reawakening memories of her first early days with Joe that Winnie hadn't thought of in years.

Jennie Tudor had a natural gift for marrying honest lyrics with gorgeous, emotional melodies. And Mike and Jennie's voices together, perfectly harmonizing Jennie's songs, created that kind of magic some musicians had a gift for, the kind that gave them lifelong fans who hungered for their next creation.

Two Decembers ago, Vic Barr spent a weekend at

one of the high-end resorts in the Tucson foothills where he heard Jennie and Mike Tudor singing in the lounge.

Vic approached them in between sets, gushing over their music. He gave them his business card: Vic Barr, TalOpps International, Talent Liaison for Film and Television. The card showed a Los Angeles address and phone number.

Barr stayed after their last set and the three of them talked deep into the night: about all the opportunities Barr could unlock for them in his hometown of L.A. About his successes representing big-name artists—he showed Jennie and Mike pictures of him posing with his clients at the Grammys—and he laid out a future for them that Jennie and Mike had long ago given up dreaming about.

What musician wouldn't want to hear that her songs belonged in movies and television, and that this man who just happened to be in the right place at the right time was exactly who they needed to make all of the right connections?

Jennie and Mike weren't stupid. They knew better than to sign just any contract. They were also savvy enough to question each other: Are we just starstruck? Are we doing the right thing?

But the risk seemed low. Vic Barr promised them that he would only take a percentage of whatever income he could generate. "It costs you nothing," he told them. "Trust me."

In Winnie's experience, always dangerous words from a stranger.

"As you will see," Rose told the jury, "the defendant was not someone to be trusted. And instead of it costing Jennie and Mike nothing, it cost them everything. That is why we are here in front of you today, ladies and gentlemen. After you hear the evidence, we ask that you return to Jennie and Mike everything the defendant has taken. You are the ones who can right this wrong. Thank you."

Rose returned to her seat. Jennie Tudor leaned over and whispered something. Rose smiled and nodded. Mike Tudor wrote something on a notepad and passed it to her. Rose answered it and passed it back.

Winnie saw all of it out of her peripheral vision. She was more interested in Judge McCracken.

He was scribbling on his own notepad again. Short marks with his pen, concentrated in one spot. If he were writing, his pen would move laterally across the page. Winnie assumed he was drawing something instead.

But she didn't have to assume it.

Winnie concentrated on the judge's hand. She let herself feel the movements in her mind. A curved line here. A long line there. Lines coming to a point. Another curve.

Winnie knew people who trained themselves to read

upside down what people sitting across from them were writing. It was a little like lip reading: interpreting the motions and translating them into words in their minds.

Winnie let her own mind go into a kind of relaxed lull. She softened her gaze and watched the judge's pen scritch on the page, while her mind translated the movements into shapes.

Winnie always carried a small spiral notebook with her. It was easier to make quick notes on it than to turn on her phone, find the note app, type and maybe retype when the words didn't come out accurately.

Easier to just use paper and pen to write what she really meant.

Or to draw some image in her mind.

Winnie took out her notebook and pen now. She kept her eyes on the judge's hand while her own hand duplicated the movements. And soon, she felt the connection click in. She didn't have to stare at his hand anymore. Her own hand was channeling the drawing on his pad. Winnie didn't have to direct it. Her hand moved the pen where it needed to go.

And while her hand moved, and the judge's hand drew, Winnie watched the shape of the judge's aura.

The first sign was a jagged distortion at his left temple.

Then a sharp bulge near his right cheek.

And then, like metal obeying the pull of a magnet, within less than a minute the judge's aura drew to it a hundred needles, both the small ones and the larger skewers. Winnie's hand moved rapidly. She felt she had to finish this sketch. But it was the judge whose hand had sped up, it was the judge who felt so urgent.

Alan Beasley was in the middle of his own opening statement. His voice had an unpleasant droning rhythm to it. Enough to make anyone fall asleep.

Judge McCracken suddenly formed a fist and pounded it once against his desk. The needles piercing his aura jumped, but they didn't retract. Winnie could see the dark blood red of the wounds jiggling beneath their tips.

The judge coughed. Coughed again. Beasley had already paused when the judge pounded the desk, and now he waited, clearly rattled, to see what might happen next.

Felicia the bailiff stepped toward the bench and asked something in a quiet voice that Winnie couldn't hear.

"It's fine!" the judge answered, but he coughed again, then again, and Winnie saw him struggling to clear his throat. It was no wonder: there was one long thin needle sticking right in the center, piercing his Adam's apple. Felicia handed the judge a cup of water. He gulped it down hard. Nothing was right.

Rose swiveled in her chair to look at Winnie. Rose looked worried, and rightfully so. Winnie held up her notepad. Then she took out her phone from the gray quilt purse and without waiting to power it on, pantomimed taking a picture of her picture. Winnie mouthed, *"Show him."*

While she waited for her phone to power on, Winnie looked back at the judge. But someone else was watching her: Felicia the bailiff locked eyes with Winnie and then shook her head. Sternly. What was Winnie doing signaling one of the attorneys? What was she doing with her phone?

Between the judge's coughing fit and this random old lady acting out of order, Felicia must have felt she was losing her grip on the courtroom.

"Recess," Judge McCracken managed to gasp. Felicia whipped around to attend to him. The judge pushed out of his chair and continued his violent coughing as he made his way out the private exit of his courtroom.

Although she must have been terribly concerned about the judge, his bailiff was professional enough to carry on with her own duties.

"Ladies and gentlemen," she told the jury, "if you'll follow me…"

Winnie could see on the jurors' faces and in their body language how rattled they all were. This wasn't how a trial looked on TV. Judges usually sat like furniture in the background. Maybe in a dramatic scene they might pound their gavel or shout, "Order!" or "Sustained!" but they didn't have lives of their own or medical issues of their own. They didn't cough and gasp and have to stumble off the bench.

Vic Barr had the sense to wait until the jurors were out of the courtroom before he yelled at his lawyer, "What the hell was that?!"

Beasley, who looked as rattled as the jurors, mumbled something to the slimeball.

"If that geezer's gonna die and I have come back here…" Barr let out a curse. "*Do* something," he told Beasley. "What are you for?"

Barr jerked to his feet and fished his phone out of his suit pocket and made a great show of storming past the benches in the back and out of the courtroom.

Winnie watched his performance. She doubted his phone had time to power on before he pressed it against his ear and pretended to be talking. "Better have good news—" he snapped at someone or no one. As he passed her Winnie smelled the rotting garbage again, along with an overpowering fog of halitosis. Barr shoved his way out the heavy wooden door, still barking into his phone. He was clearly a very important man. Very busy. Or at least that was the impression he wanted to give.

But Winnie saw something else entirely:

It was summer somewhere. Bright sunlight streamed through the flimsy curtains of a cheap-looking, seedy motel room.

Vic Barr sat on top of an unmade bed wearing a dingy

T-shirt, yellow at the armpits, and a ratty old pair of gym shorts. He held his phone to his ear.

He was in a hurry again, but this time he sounded excited and cheerful, not angry.

"I'm in the lobby at Universal right now," he lied. "They're about to pull me into a meeting." He held his hand loosely over the phone and pretended to talk to someone else. "Yeah, thanks, love. Tell them I'll be right in. No, just a water. Thanks."

Whoever Barr was talking to in real life on the other end of his phone must have asked a question. "They loved it," Barr said. "Especially *Tell Me Again*. Said it's perfect for something they've got in post-production." Barr chuckled. "I know. I told you. Did I tell you?"

He picked at a loose nylon thread on the brown and orange paisley bedspread while he listened to the response. "Yeah," he said next, "so I need you to sign and scan those pages and send them to me right away. Next two minutes. They said they won't talk to me unless I have them."

Another question from the person on the other end of the call.

"I know, it's just their forms." Winnie could see the sweat slicking on Barr's face. She could smell it, too, as strongly as if she were stuck in an elevator with him: dirty feet, dirty armpits, unwashed sheets and dirty clothes. "Lawyer stuff," Barr said, "whatever. Don't worry about it. It's just so we can make a deal. This is it. I can feel it."

Winnie could hear someone exclaiming with excitement on the other end. A woman.

Jennie Tudor? Winnie couldn't be sure. It made sense that it would be. Otherwise why would Winnie's mind show her this particular scene?

"Okay, yep! I gotta go. They're calling me in. Send me the contract right away. Let's do this!"

Barr ended the call. He blew out a stale breath. He dropped his phone on the motel mattress and flopped backward onto the pillows.

Winnie's view of the scene changed. She was looking right down on the slimeball now and could see the satisfaction on his face. A sick kind of delight.

With one hand he scratched himself somewhere Winnie didn't need to see, and with the other he picked up his phone and checked it.

"Yess..." he whispered as he clicked on an email. He thumbed through it and smiled. "Good girl."

Then he sat up and reached for the beer can sweating on the table beside the bed. Out the window Winnie saw someone pass by on their way to another room. She still had no idea where Barr was—but it certainly wasn't in the lobby of Universal. He wasn't in a meeting with anyone to discuss Jennie Tudor's music.

Winnie widened her view to search for any kind of

clues in the room. A notepad, maybe, with the motel name on it—there was a pad by the bed, but the motel hadn't sprung for having it specially printed with their name.

Something else...

Winnie tried to see out the flimsy curtains, to find any kind of motel sign outside. All she saw were palm trees. But at least that was some kind of clue.

Then finally she got a hit. It had been covered by the edge of the bedspread, but now that Barr shifted to sit up against the chipped headboard and savor his beer, he kicked the bedspread further away and exposed the embossed three-ring binder that came with the room. The kind Winnie assumed had information about check-out time and maybe even a few nearby restaurants that delivered. The place didn't seem nice enough to rate its own attached diner.

On the cover of the binder was the motel name and logo. Winnie recognized it from TV shows she had seen. She always assumed it was fictional with its over-the-top kitschy name, but here it was, a real place after all.

Barr took a long chug of his beer. He burped. This was the class act Winnie had seen at the courthouse this morning with his shiny leather shoes and expensive-looking suit and dye job. Now that she looked more closely at him in the motel room, she could see the gray stripe of his real hair color growing back in along his part, and the patches of gray sprouting at his temples. His hair might have looked fine in its natural state, going totally gray, but Barr obviously wanted to make a more youthful impression.

But no matter how he dressed himself up for court this morning, he was still who he was at his core. A liar. A con man. Winnie had no doubt the contract Barr pressured Jennie Tudor to sign and send—just as a "formality"—was exactly the one Rose showed her last night, assigning all of Jennie's rights in her entire music catalog to Vic Barr's business.

That was the difficulty of Rose's case: Jennie and Mike Tudor did in fact sign the contract. Barr didn't have to forge their names, he just had to lie to them.

And now it was up to Rose to convince the jury they should disregard the contract and rule that Vic Barr was liable for fraud.

Otherwise everything Jennie and Mike had worked for over the decades—all of their beautiful music—now belonged to the sleezeball Barr. He could even demand that Jennie and Mike pay him for every gig where they played their own songs. They didn't own the rights anymore. Pay up.

Winnie was tired of looking at Barr in his slovenly clothes and his pigsty room. More than that, she was tired of smelling him. It was as if someone were holding a dirty tennis shoe right over her face. She wondered how long it would take for the reek of Vic Barr to entirely leave her nose.

Winnie's mind obeyed. The images faded away. She felt herself solidly back inside the courtroom sitting on the padded bench. But she took another moment to process what she had just seen. She opened her notebook and quickly wrote down the conversation she'd over-heard. She would transcribe it in a text to Rose and see if it might help.

The judge's bailiff returned to the courtroom. "Judge McCracken says we will reconvene after lunch," she told Rose and Beasley. "Be back here at one-fifteen."

"Is he all right?" Rose asked.

"He's fine," Felicia answered, her tone clipped. Obvi-ously she wasn't going to discuss the judge's personal matters with the attorneys.

But Winnie could see the change in Felicia's aura. This morning it had been a lively mix of rose and orange, but now it was mostly dark brown. A band of lighter beige encircled her chest. Winnie saw it, but didn't know what to make of it, only that there was a change.

Alan Beasley gathered his papers and slid them into his briefcase. He didn't speak to Rose. His client was already somewhere else. Beasley looked glum as he ambled past Winnie and slouched over his phone.

Now that they had the courtroom to themselves, Winnie realized how odd it looked for her still to be sitting there. She slipped her notebook back into her purse and quietly left Rose with her clients. Winnie planned to position herself back near the restrooms again where she could wait for Rose to come out.

At least that had been her plan.

But the stench of Vic Barr was so overpowering as soon as she came out into the hall, Winnie had to sit down on the nearest bench.

He was over near the windows, making a big show of being a big man and giving his lawyer a proper dressing down. Spittle flew from Barr's lips as he railed in a kind of shouting whisper. Winnie heard some of the words he emphasized, in between the swearing: "...—ing in*compe-tent* ... paid you *money* ... shoulda *jumped* on it ... I want a *mis*trial..."

Beasley looked miserable. Winnie saw the contractor with the bushy beard watching them as he waited for an elevator.

Beasley saw him, too.

He mumbled something to Barr, no doubt warning him to keep his voice down while jurors were still around.

"Don't tell *me* to shut up," Barr answered. He ran his right hand through his hair, ruining whatever style he'd given it earlier. Once his hand was free again he jabbed his index finger into Alan Beasley's chest. "*Fix* this"—jab —"Get me *out* of it"—jab—"Do your"—expletive—"*job*."

But Beasley was not as intimidated as Barr must have

expected. In fact, Winnie saw him add a few inches to his height by actually standing up straight. When he wasn't slouching Beasley looked impressively tall.

Maybe Barr had finally crossed the line by actually putting his hand on his lawyer. But whatever the reason, Beasley looked about done.

"We can talk about this outside," he said calmly. Then he turned and headed for the elevators.

Barr barked after him, "Just *do* it."

But Beasley had snapped his leash, it looked like to Winnie, and whatever had gone on between him and his client before now, he was obviously tired of just going along.

And oh, the smell Barr's tantrum created: like burnt rubber mixed with dirty underwear and rancid meat.

Winnie covered her nose. The stench was overpowering. She couldn't understand why everyone in the area wasn't giving Barr wide berth.

Rose and the Tudors were out of the courtroom now. Rose widened her eyes at Winnie, who kept her hand over her nose and shook her head. Barr was poison.

Rose and the Tudors hung back while they waited for Barr to catch the next elevator. Then Rose told her clients, "I have some calls to return. I'll see you both after lunch. Text me if you think of any questions."

Rose waited for Jennie and Mike to disappear into one

of the elevators, then she sank down onto the wooden bench next to Winnie.

"Wow. So that's a morning," Rose said.

Winnie patted her niece's knee.

"Does he smell to you?" Rose asked.

"You can't even imagine," Winnie said. "It makes my eyes water."

"So what does that mean?"

"It means I'm going to do everything I can to help you win this. But first I have to tell you about the judge."

8

Rose bought sandwiches at a deli near the courthouse—turkey and Swiss for her, grilled portobello mushroom and Havarti for Winnie—and they sat in Rose's Volvo in the underground parking garage where they could talk and eat in private.

Winnie told her everything she had seen, only briefly skimming over the woman in gray's substitution of pages in someone's will. Winnie had more important things to report.

She described everything she saw about the horrible state of Judge McCracken's aura. And about the energy leaking out—pouring out in places—that might be putting his life in danger at this very moment.

"I drew this," Winnie said, showing her the sketches she copied as the judge made them himself.

There were three of them.

"He's better at drawing than I am," Winnie said. "But these will give you an idea."

There was a seascape: shore and sky, a cluster of large rocks at the edge of the beach, the curve of seagulls' wings in the distance, clouds paralleling the water.

Another sea image: this time of a whale's tail breaching between waves. More clouds this time, a sense of drama about the sky and water, as if there might be a storm.

And last: a similar-looking whale's tail, but this one at the end of a bracelet, serving as a form of clasp. The bracelet looked braided, and ended in a loop. The tail fit neatly inside the loop to complete the circle.

Winnie thought of the photo she and Rose found on the internet last night of William and Helen McCracken smiling on the deck of a cruise ship.

This was how the judge doodled during jury selection. His mind was far away from the business at hand.

But what bothered Winnie was that his daydreaming and doodling actually appeared to make him worse. It was during those distractions that the needles and skewers attacked.

"He makes them go away when he shouts," Winnie told Rose. "Remember when he pounded his fist? It was because of the needles. They were obviously hurting him at some deep level. I'm sure yelling at you and Alan

Beasley helps him. Probably fining you both fifteen hundred dollars felt good, at least for a moment."

Rose scowled. "I'm not going to say I hope that helped. I wrote the check myself. Didn't feel good to me."

"No. I looked at his bailiff when she came out after his coughing fit. She's not happy. No one is happy. He can't go on this way."

Rose unwrapped the chocolate chip cookie she bought at the deli for them to split. She broke it in half and left Winnie's portion inside its cellophane.

"I don't know what to do with any of this," Rose said, sampling her cookie. "I believe you that he's in danger. I believe all of this. But I don't know how to help him and I don't know how to help Jennie and Mike beyond doing my best with their case. I'm open to any suggestions you have."

Winnie realized she had forgotten to tell Rose all about Vic Barr. She ate her half of the cookie while she relayed the scene in the motel room.

"Snake," Rose said after hearing it all. "I mean, we knew he lied, but there you have it. What a crook."

"Ask Jennie if she remembers that specific conversa-tion," Winnie said. "Maybe she can tell us more."

Rose wiped her hands on a napkin and thumbed out a text to Jennie Tudor. She showed it to Winnie before she sent it.

Do you remember Barr saying he was at Universal to discuss Tell Me Again?

The answer came back swiftly:

What's Tell Me Again?

Winnie and Rose looked at each other. Then Rose's thumbs flew.

That's not your song?

No. What are we talking about?

Winnie wasn't as fast as Rose with typing on her phone, but she got the job done. A quick search of the song title. She showed her phone screen to Rose, who immediately texted Jennie.

Do you know someone named Sabrina Rich?

Winnie typed another search onto her phone.

No, came Jennie's answer.

But Winnie's research produced a hit.
She showed it to Rose. Rose shook her head.

"Slimeball." They both continued typing on their phones. Not exactly the old days of using a card catalog at a library, Winnie thought. She liked this much, much better.

Rose checked her watch. "We have to get back." But first she called her legal assistant, Crystal, back at the office. Rose gave her a set of instructions. "Text my Aunt Winnie as soon as you get it," Rose said. She recited Winnie's phone number. "Thanks, Crys. Do it as fast as you can."

Winnie wasn't waiting. She continued doing research on her phone. Her heart was racing. She was on the hunt now. She could smell her prey—boy, could she.

She looked forward to never having to smell him again.

"We have to go," Rose said. They balled up their garbage and gathered purse and briefcase and left the parking garage separately.

Maybe it didn't matter if they still pretended not to know each other. Winnie wasn't sure. But they had come this far in their clandestine precautions, so why not see them through all the way to the end?

Winnie gave Rose a long head start before following her outside the parking garage, down the sidewalk, and up the series of concrete steps to the courthouse.

Off to her right, in the shadows of the administrative office building next door, she could make out the slouching figure of Alan Beasley. He was talking on his phone.

From this distance, Winnie couldn't see his face, but she could see his posture: he looked defeated.

More than that, she could see the swirling cloud of yellow and gray surrounding his body. The aura of a man in the midst of some kind of turmoil, whether mental or emotional or physical, she couldn't say.

But her flashlight was on now. She did not just stand in a dark warehouse wondering where she was or where to go next.

Winnie did not make a habit out of listening in to people's private phone calls, but she made an exception. This was too important. Vic Barr was a con man who had stolen a hard-working couple's livelihood. He robbed a gifted musician of her art. Winnie did not feel conflicted at all about hearing what Beasley might reveal about his client.

But she was too late. The lawyer ended his call and stood motionless—physically, at least, although his aura was anything but inactive. It swirled in ever-increasing waves of gray and pale dirty yellow, like the judge's sketch of stormy seas turned on its side.

Since there was nothing more to discover about the call, Winnie returned her attention to her footing as she continued climbing up the wide concrete steps. She couldn't allow herself to be so distracted she might miss a step and trip.

And then as she passed by the fountain, the smell hit her again. It was as though she had just crossed over some barrier between a world filled with fresh clean winter air into a rat-infested tunnel filling up with sewage.

Winnie turned away sharply and covered her nose. She had to fight the urge to gag. Her lunch threatened to come back up.

This time the stench wasn't just in her nose, it had invaded her mouth and throat. She could smell it, she could *taste* it. Horrible. Vile. A thick fog of nauseating fumes. She wasn't just breathing it in, she felt like she was drowning in it.

And what she told Rose before was true: it made her eyes water. For a moment her vision blurred.

But she saw enough to know that Vic Barr had just passed her on the steps, reeking of aggression and filth, on his way to confront his lawyer.

The worst of the fumes moved with him. Winnie slowed her ascent. She drew in several clean breaths. And she listened. She wanted to just stand in place and watch, but she knew they might notice her then. Beasley seemed to be aware of his surroundings. He had noticed the juror with the bushy beard watching them before.

While Winnie pretended to stop and search for something in her quilted purse, she took some pleasure in overhearing Alan Beasley say no. And then no twice more. Whatever the slimeball was trying to make him do, Beasley continued refusing.

Good for you, Winnie thought. Maybe a C-student, but not a spineless one. She felt new respect for Rose's opponent.

Then Winnie's phone dinged. A text from Rose's legal assistant, Crystal.

Winnie stood reading it on the steps and smiled.

9

Crystal the legal assistant had included Rose in the group text, but if Rose were back in the courtroom already she might have had to turn her phone off.

Winnie wanted to bring her the information as soon as possible, but she also needed to do a little more research on her own.

Her phone dinged.

Outstanding, Rose texted Crystal.

So she had been able to read it after all.

Winnie felt less urgency now about joining Rose in the courtroom. She knew her time would be better spent sitting someplace alone where she could quiet her mind and ask it to show her more.

Now that Crystal found out the date of the conversation...

Now that Winnie's research had told her more about Sabrina Rich...

There was a point at which even the best researcher would be able to uncover only a certain number of facts.

But Winnie had greater resources than the internet. She had an entire database of information and history at her disposal. She just needed to know where to focus her attention. She needed to know what to ask.

Maybe another clairvoyant would approach this puzzle differently. Winnie could only do it the way that worked best for her.

So she sat down on the edge of one of the concrete planters in front of the courthouse. Even though she would have preferred sitting in the sunlight and grabbing its warmth, Winnie chose a less conspicuous spot in the shade. She wished her coat and pants were both a little thicker to provide more insulation from the cold concrete. The Saguaro cactus standing tall in its gravel bed behind her probably also wished it could bask in some sun.

Winnie set her gray quilted purse on her lap, folded her hands over it, and closed her eyes.

There were times in her life when images sprang into her mind on their own. Like with the potential juror this morning, the woman in gray who swapped out the pages in somebody's will. Or like seeing Vic Barr inside that seedy motel room. Winnie didn't know enough about him to ask to see such a thing. Her mind just furnished it because there were things it wanted her to know.

Winnie had learned over the years to treat her clairvoyance like a partnership. Sometimes it acted on its own, supplying information she needed to have—even if she didn't immediately understand why—and sometimes Winnie was the instigator, prompting the images and knowledge to come to her mind because she asked.

Winnie sat in the cold winter shade she shared with the tall silent cactus and this time she specifically asked.

Victor Barr and Sabrina Rich. Show me.

10

W innie thought about writing out her notes by hand, but then the next action stymied her: how would she get the notes to Rose inside the courtroom? Winnie couldn't just walk up to the little fence separating the public seating from all the litigants—could she?

What would Judge McCracken say to that? He had already indulged the little old white-haired lady who needed a place to wait until her friend picked her up in the afternoon. Winnie doubted he would be so accommodating of a little old lady passing notes to one of the attorneys. It would be worse than having a teacher catch her passing notes to a friend in school.

But if she texted the information to Rose, there was no guarantee Rose would see it. The bailiff had instructed everyone inside the courtroom to turn off their phones once the case officially began. Everyone could turn them back on during breaks, but Winnie could imagine what Judge McCracken would say if someone's phone pinged or rang or even just vibrated while court was in session. In his current state, he might hit the roof.

Oh.

The image sprang into Winnie's mind, as answers so often did: Rose and Beasley looking at their computer tablets this morning after the judge demanded they hurry up and pick their jury. The names of the potential jurors were on those tablets, not on a printed list.

Which meant that the lawyers were allowed to keep their tablets powered on during trial. They probably just had to mute any sound.

Winnie did not consider herself a technological wizard, but she knew the basics. She had a tablet at home, too, and knew that texts that were sent to her phone also showed up on her tablet.

So she could write out all her new information in a text and get it to Rose that way. Winnie just had to make sure that Rose knew to look.

After sitting in the cold shade for the past ten minutes, Winnie needed warmth again and sunlight. She looked around to make sure both Beasley and Barr were gone. Then she stood in the blessed sunshine and quietly began dictating into her phone everything she just learned.

The key was to organize it so that Rose could get to the important details quickly. Winnie did not have the luxury of telling Rose the whole story, the way she could when they ate their lunch in the car.

Who—what—where.

Winnie dictated the relevant information so Rose would know why it was important.

Then she relayed the juiciest information. The kind she knew would make Rose sit up straight and pay attention.

Winnie reviewed her long text to make sure it gave Rose what she needed. Satisfied, she hit send.

Then she hurried back inside the courthouse, knowing her next challenge was to get Rose to read the text.

Up on the sixth floor there were far fewer people milling around than this morning. Winnie listened at the door to the courtroom. But it was so thick she couldn't hear whether any sounds were coming from inside.

She cautiously opened the door. The trial was already back in session. The judge sat behind his desk on the platform, the jury sat in the jury box, and Alan Beasley was telling them his version of the case. The judge's coughing fit had interrupted Beasley's opening statement this morning. Barr's lawyer must have picked it up where he left off.

Judge McCracken did not look pleased to see Winnie

again. She couldn't help that. She needed to be there. For Rose's sake and for the Tudors'.

Rose must have been waiting for her to return, because as Winnie sat down again in the last row of padded benches, Rose swiveled in her chair and made eye contact.

Winnie made a show of taking her cell phone out of her purse, pointing to the screen, then pretending she just remembered to turn it off. Before she put it back in her purse she pointed at the screen again. She didn't know how else to signal Rose.

Winnie watched and waited, hoping Rose got the message.

Rose obviously understood at least as much technology as Winnie did, because she casually picked up her tablet and pressed the screen in a few places.

Winnie relaxed. Message received.

Now she watched Rose read her text. Alan Beasley droned on.

Winnie wasn't paying much attention to him, until she realized Beasley kept using one particular word.

When Rose gave her opening statement, she told the Tudors' story with complete confidence and conviction. The Tudors did this ... the defendant did that ... the defendant committed fraud like this.

But Beasley, for whatever reason, was hedging.

"My client claims he didn't say that..."

"Mr. Barr claims the Tudors were fully informed..."

Claims.

Winnie thought it was an odd word to use.

As if Alan Beasley didn't believe his client himself.

She wondered if he would have given a different opening statement this morning before his blow-up with Barr.

She continued listening to Beasley, but she kept her gaze on the judge.

He seemed more attentive than this morning. Good. Winnie suspected it was when his mind wandered that the aura started attracting the needles.

A few minutes later, Beasley wrapped up his opening statement. Nothing remarkable, just what sounded like a They Said-He Said kind of case. The Tudors alleged Barr was a crook, Barr said he wasn't.

Correction: Barr *claimed* he did nothing wrong.

Was using that word intentional? It had to be. Maybe Alan Beasley wanted to make sure Judge McCracken didn't blame him for presenting Barr's lies to the court.

Was that how it worked? Like crossing your fingers behind your back? You could knowingly let your client lie, as long as you were careful not to say you believed it?

Winnie wanted so much to ask Rose that question. She would know. But Rose was busy calling her first witness.

Jennie Tudor made her way stiffly toward the front.

She looked terrified. She wore plain black pants, black boots, and a pretty coral sweater. She wasn't rich, you could see that in what both of the Tudors wore. Mike wore black jeans, black cowboy boots, and a button-down shirt under a jacket. No tie. Winnie wondered if he even owned one. There was such a thing as "Tucson casual," and one feature was a distinct absence of ties.

Now that she noticed it, she looked at the jury. Four men, and not a single one wearing a tie. Winter jackets, but no sports coats or suits. Winnie didn't like to dress up, either. She had no quarrel with comfortable clothing.

As Jennie Tudor raised her right hand and repeated the oath the court clerk read off a notecard—the same oath Winnie had heard countless times on TV shows and in movies: "I swear to tell the truth, the whole truth, and nothing but the truth"—she could imagine what Jennie must look like when she was in a ballroom or on a stage somewhere performing instead of testifying.

And then Winnie didn't have to imagine it. She saw it. Jennie on keyboard, singing harmony with Mike. Jennie wore satin-looking pants with colorful rhinestones down the sides. On top she wore a bright glittery teal top. Her long brown hair was loose and wavy. She looked stunning. And she looked joyful, singing her own music.

While Jennie played an electric keyboard, Mike sat perched on a stool beside her strumming his guitar. They both looked at each other, smiling as they harmonized Jennie's beautiful love song.

Winnie wished she could sit and listen to them longer. See the joy on their faces instead of this stress. Maybe after this was all over she and Rose could go hear them one evening.

But first the Tudors needed to take back all of Jennie's music from the leech sitting in the courtroom glaring at Jennie Tudor right now.

The smell invaded Winnie's nostrils. A new rank scent, like something dead and decaying. She covered her nose. Barr's wretched aura was intolerable. The sooner this was all over, the better.

Jennie Tudor sat on the witness seat with her spine erect and shoulders so tight they were nearly up to her ear lobes.

Winnie knew she was biased, but she couldn't help being impressed with how calm, patient, and methodical Rose was in asking Jennie her questions. Little by little, Jennie was able to tell the jury her whole story: from her childhood dreams of becoming a musician, to meeting her husband their freshman year of high school, to marrying and raising a family while also taking a chance on their music careers.

"And then you met the defendant." Rose said with the same sympathetic tone as if someone might say, *And then you had the car accident.* Or *Then the war came.* Some unfortunate calamity out of Jennie's and Mike's control.

Jennie still looked too nervous to address herself to the jury. She kept her eyes on Rose and answered every question.

But Rose looked at the women and men seated in the jury box as if she always wanted to include them in the conversation. "What else did he promise?" she asked, keeping her body turned halfway between Jennie and the jury. "What else did he say?" Bit by bit, the whole sordid story came out.

"Can you tell the jury, in your own words," Rose prompted her gently. "How did it feel when you heard your song in that movie?"

Winnie saw the pain on Jennie's face. Tears gathered in her eyes. "I was..." Jennie's hand shook as she covered her mouth, trying to keep from making any noise as she fought back her tears. "...proud," Jennie continued. She managed to smile, but that, too, looked shot through with pain. "It was ... our dream, you know?" For the first time she shifted her gaze away from Rose and connected with the strangers on the jury. "To hear one of my songs, to hear Mike and me singing it..." And now a sound did escape, a singular sob. Jennie bowed her head and pressed her hand over her mouth.

Rose pulled a tissue out of the box sitting on the edge

of the plaintiffs' table. She handed it to Jennie, who discreetly wiped beneath her nose.

"Tell us, Jennie," Rose said softly. "Why are you crying?"

"Because..." Jennie looked up at her with tear-filled eyes. "We didn't own it anymore."

"Did you intend to sign away all your rights to your music?" Rose asked.

"No! He said it was just a formality—"

Winnie's skin tingled at hearing that exact phrase again.

Rose asked Jennie just a few more questions. Then it was Alan Beasley's turn to cross-examine her.

It went just as Winnie expected. Just as Rose had warned her would happen. "It's how I'd play it if I represented Barr," Rose had explained the night before. "That contract is pretty clear. They signed it. In a lot of ways, it looks like an open and shut case."

"But he lied to them," Winnie said.

"Lied and lied," Rose agreed. "I just need the jury to see that."

Winnie watched the jurors now, to try to gauge how they felt about Beasley's questions and Jennie's answers.

Winnie could see Beasley was scoring some points. He brought in a huge posterboard with the contract blown up on it. The words were right there: *All rights.*

"Is that your signature?" Beasley asked her.

"Yes." Jennie couldn't look at him when she said it.

"Is that your husband's signature?"

"Yes."

Alan Beasley turned to the judge. "That's all I have, your honor."

"Next witness," Judge McCracken ordered. He seemed subdued, a little lethargic, but otherwise not in immediate peril. Winnie could see the same pale blue aura lightly pulsating around him, and noticed several more rips in it than she remembered from this morning, but at least the needles were gone. For now. Judge McCracken was maintaining.

"We call Victor Barr," Rose said in her clear, confident voice.

Beasley seemed surprised. Maybe he expected Mike Tudor to go next. But Vic Barr stood up from his table as if he loved any attention, and made his way to the witness box.

He repeated the oath about telling the truth, and then settled himself into the seat. Winnie watched puffs of acid green pop all around him. She glanced at the jury to see if anyone noticed any stench. The jurors looked curious about this new player on the scene. No one seemed offended by the scent of a rotting carcass.

Rose stood for a moment studying a sheet of paper in her hand. Winnie wondered if it was the affidavit Crystal had texted the two of them a short time ago.

Rose must have asked the court clerk to print it out for her.

But the question Rose asked could not be on that affidavit.

The information had come from Winnie herself.

"Mr. Barr, on June twelfth, four years ago, were you a guest at the Sin City Sun Fun Beach Motel in Las Vegas, Nevada?"

"Um ... where?" Barr seemed confused. Clearly this was not the question he expected. But Winnie saw something else: a vague sense of alarm.

Barr glanced worriedly over at his lawyer, but Beasley was busy writing something on his legal pad.

Rose repeated her question.

"Uh ... I don't really know," Barr said.

Rose referred to her sheet of paper again. "If the records from Sin City Sun Fun Beach Motel list you as a guest on that date, would you agree they are accurate?"

Barr's look of alarm was growing. Again he tried to catch his lawyer's eye. Again Beasley ignored him and continued writing.

"Yes or no," Rose said firmly, but not unpleasantly.

But Barr just kept glancing from Rose to Beasley, back to Rose, obviously hoping for some kind of intervention.

Judge McCracken was losing whatever patience he might still have. "Answer the question," he snarled.

Now the jury was paying attention. People were

leaning forward in their chairs. Winnie understood perfectly. Finally this was more like TV. Clearly the red-haired lawyer was about to spring some trap.

And the growing sheen of sweat on Barr's face was making him look more and more like a guilty man who needed to be caught.

But he was slick, or at least he thought he was. "I don't remember. That was a long time ago."

"That's fine," Rose said. "Credit card charges and motel records can be provided."

Winnie admired the way Rose walked this particular line. She didn't lie, didn't exaggerate what evidence she currently had in her possession. Maybe Barr and everyone else would assume the proof was on the sheet of paper in Rose's hand. But Rose chose her words carefully: *If the records list you ... records can be provided...*

Rose glanced at the mysterious paper once again.

"What is the name of your company?" she asked.

Barr instantly relaxed back into his smug demeanor. Rose obviously had nothing on him. All he had to do was deny he remembered the motel, and she had no choice but to move on to some other—and much easier—question.

Barr pointed at the enlarged contract on the poster-board still set up where the jury could see it. "TalentOpps. Just like it says there."

"Do you also own a company called TalentEst?" Rose asked.

Barr's mouth slacked open in surprise. He stared at Rose. Winnie could see him calculating how best to answer as acid-green puffs furiously burst all around him. The stench of rotting meat reached her all the way at the back of the courtroom.

"Talent ... Est," Barr said, as if he had only just heard the name for the first time right now. Winnie wondered if the jury could see he was stalling. "Uh, yeah. I do," he admitted, smiling bashfully as if he just remembered. "It's not active right now, but..." Barr shrugged. He glanced over at Beasley, obviously still hoping for some help. But Beasley was too busy writing notes to himself.

People on the jury were still paying attention. They didn't understand where this was all going, but it looked like it could be interesting.

Rose picked up two more sheets of paper from her table. She handed one to Judge McCracken and the other to Alan Beasley.

Winnie loved watching how Rose played it. The jurors looked more intrigued than ever. Winnie saw all of them looking back and forth between Beasley and the judge, waiting for some reaction from whatever it was they were reading.

What was on that paper? What was this new secret? Vic Barr was still smiling, trying to seem unconcerned, but maybe some of them noticed a creeping look of discomfort on his face.

Then Rose set the hook.

"Are you familiar with the name Sabrina Rich?"

Barr's pasted-on smile vanished. "What?"

"Sabrina Rich," Rose repeated. "Do you know her?"

"What? I..." Barr looked at his lawyer. Beasley set down the sheet of paper and leaned back in his chair. He seemed mildly interested in Rose's question. He made no effort to interfere.

"Is Sabrina Rich a singer and songwriter?" Rose asked.

Winnie saw several more members of the jury lean forward in their chairs. All of them were paying close attention. Winnie was glad to see that the judge was, too. For the moment his pale blue aura pulsated softly around him. No needles. No skewers. No pain.

Long ago, when Rose was first starting out as a lawyer, she told Winnie that one of her bosses had schooled her that day in basic litigation strategy: *Never ask a question during trial that you don't already know the answer to.* Rose told Winnie numerous stories over the years of disasters caused by not following that advice, and victories when she did.

Rose already knew the answer to the question she asked Vic Barr. Yet he continued to just stare back at her, as if by not answering he could somehow avoid it.

"Mr. Barr?" Rose prompted.

Barr looked at his lawyer again, practically begging him with his laser gaze to say something—make an objection—*do* something.

"Answer the question," Judge McCracken snapped.

Barr nodded.

"Out loud," Judge McCracken growled.

"Yes," Barr said.

"Did you represent Sabrina Rich through your company TalentEst?"

Sweat glistened on Barr's face. Just as Winnie had seen in the seedy motel room while Barr was lying to the woman on the phone. The woman Winnie now knew was not Jennie Tudor, but was Sabrina Rich.

Barr nodded. He caught himself and answered audibly, "Yes. But that has nothing to do with this." He glared at Alan Beasley. Beasley stayed seated and silent. Winnie could not see his face, but she guessed it was perfectly bland. Beasley was not going to help his client. Not now, maybe not anymore.

"Plaintiffs submit the affidavit of Sabrina Rich," Rose told the judge. "We only learned of her today, so we are unable to have her appear here at trial, but if the court needs to hear from her personally..."

"No objection," Alan Beasley said.

"No *objection*?" Barr said.

Winnie could imagine all the hateful things Barr would say to his lawyer right now if they were alone. His threats and his cursing. Winnie couldn't wait to ask Rose later if what Beasley was doing was allowed. He seemed determined not to help Vic Barr lie on the stand.

"Then I will read from Ms. Rich's affidavit," Rose said.

The facts were almost exactly as Jennie Tudor had described them. A chance meeting at a resort in San Diego where Sabrina Rich performed. Promises, so many promises. Pressure to sign away all her rights to all her music, "just as a formality."

Winnie had watched that conversation as it unfolded in a rundown motel while Barr lied about meeting with executives at Universal. But now she understood it from Sabrina Rich's side. Sabrina had signed the contract, just as Jennie and Mike had signed an almost identical one. And when Barr, maybe to his own surprise, actually did find success with one of her songs, *Tell Me Again*, licensing it to a streaming series that made it a hit—Sabrina didn't own it or any of her own songs anymore. Vic Barr owned them all.

"You were not, in fact, at a meeting in Los Angeles that day, were you?" Rose asked. "You were at a motel in Las Vegas, Nevada."

"She misunderstood," Barr tried. "It was telephonic."

Rose didn't miss a beat. "Yet your phone records do not show any calls between you and anyone from Universal that day, correct?"

She said it as if she already knew. But Winnie noticed once again the careful choice of words.

Barr stared at her, obviously weighing what to do.

Judge McCracken broke in again. "Answer. Yes or no."

Barr tried to shrug it away. "I'm sorry," he told the judge. "I don't remember. That was a long time ago."

"Let's see if I can refresh your memory," Rose said, this time with a sharpness to her voice. "Four years ago, on June twelfth, you called Sabrina Rich from a motel room in Las Vegas and fraudulently represented to her that you were in Los Angeles, California, in the lobby of Universal Studios. You fraudulently represented that you were about to attend a meeting with music executives about her song *Tell Me Again*. You fraudulently told her they would not meet with you unless you showed them a signed contract stating that Sabrina Rich had assigned to you all rights to her entire music catalog. As with Jennie and Mike Tudor, you claimed this was just a formality. But as with Jennie and Mike Tudor, you fraudulently gained control of all of their musical rights, and then made your own deals with various TV streaming services. You have never shared any of the money with Sabrina Rich, or my clients, Jennie and Mike. Mr. Barr, isn't all of this correct?"

"No," he said. "That's not what happened—"

But he never finished his lie.

Because Winnie had lost sight of the judge. She had

been so absorbed by Rose's performance, she forgot to keep an eye on William McCracken.

She didn't know what changed or when it occurred. The last time she looked at him, he seemed fine. But he must have fallen into some kind of lull again, let himself relax too much, because when Winnie looked at him now his entire aura bristled with more needles and skewers than ever, and his pale blue outline was a dark and bloody red.

Now not just one, but several long and lethal-looking skewers penetrated his throat. Judge McCracken gasped for air and began violently coughing.

Winnie jolted to her feet.

"Catch him!" she shouted—to Rose, to Barr, to Beasley, to anyone.

Because she could see in her mind's eye what was about to come next.

And a moment later, it occurred in real time. Judge McCracken clutched desperately at his throat and toppled from his chair.

Into the waiting arms of his sturdy bailiff.

Felicia had acted immediately when Winnie shouted for help. And now she was there to catch her boss just in time.

"Call 911!" Felicia bellowed, and other people sprang into action, and everything afterward moved as it should.

But Winnie sank to her seat, defeated.

She should have helped him sooner.

Alerted his bailiff sooner. Done something more—anything.

Because she already knew this morning that the judge was in danger. Why didn't she speak up then? Why didn't she do more than just tell Rose?

But Winnie knew the answer. Because she had faced it before. As old as she was, as wise as she liked to think she had become after all these years of learning to respect and apply her gift, she was obviously still allowing this one lingering fear to hold her back. Not always, not even often anymore. But here it was again, and she couldn't deny it.

Maybe because he was a judge, maybe because Winnie had elevated him in her mind as such a serious and impressive person, the old insecurity had crept back in:

Winnie assumed he would never believe her.

But that was no excuse. She should have tried. Because now, if Judge McCracken died, and she might have saved him while she had the chance...

Winnie watched in silent dread as the paramedics strapped an oxygen mask over his face and lifted him onto a gurney. As they wheeled him out past her, she stood to catch a glimpse of his face.

He was still alive, for now.

But for how much longer?

Winnie tried, but she couldn't see that future.

Now all anyone could do was wait.

11

Winnie sat on the couch between Clover and King Arthur, sipping lemon tea with honey. The dogs seemed to understand she needed their comfort. Clover rested her head on Winnie's lap. King Arthur lay coiled right up against her. She could feel both dogs' soft slow breaths.

Winnie felt ill. No, not ill so much as wrung out to the end of her energy. She needed to sit quietly now and try to coax it to come back.

She couldn't bear the thought of dinner. All she wanted was a warm drink she could hold between her cold hands.

"Do you want me to come home with you?" Rose had asked her. She must have seen how affected Winnie was.

"No," Winnie said. "I'll be fine. I just need to rest. You did a wonderful job today. I'm so proud of you."

They hugged in the parking garage, and then both went to their separate cars.

Winnie knew Rose must be tired to the bone herself. It had been a long, stressful day in court.

In the end Rose had introduced her clients to Winnie. Outside the courthouse Winnie shook Jennie's and Mike's hands and told them everything would be all right. Winnie believed it. Knew it. Although she couldn't exactly tell them what was next or how it would end.

Because the trial wasn't finished. And Rose wasn't certain when it would be. "We'll have to wait to see how Judge McCracken is," Rose told them. "If he survives, then…" Rose shrugged. "I don't know. We just have to see."

Alan Beasley passed by them just then and gave Rose an acknowledging nod. Winnie hadn't seen Vic Barr since pandemonium broke out in the courtroom. He seemed to have just slipped away. Beasley was probably grateful.

Winnie wondered if Barr got his mistrial after all.

What happens if a judge dies during your trial?

Winnie didn't have the heart to ask Rose about that yet. She wanted to concentrate on Judge McCracken recovering instead.

So she did that now, in the quiet of her living room, dogs snuggled up to her on either side.

She hesitated to ask, because she might not like the answer.

But she was a grown up, and death was a part of life. She knew that as well as anyone else.

"Show me," she said softly.

The scene poured into Winnie's mind. She saw Felicia the bailiff sitting beside Judge McCracken's bed in a busy, overloaded emergency room. It was hours after he must have arrived there. Why wasn't he in a proper room yet?

Felicia still wore her outfit from court. She had taken off her suit jacket and draped it over the back of her chair, but she didn't look comfortable in her button-down blouse and formal trousers and dress shoes. Normally by this time of night she was probably in sweatpants and a warm top and thick socks like Winnie wore right now.

But Winnie had pegged the judge's bailiff right from the start: Loyal. Reliable. Honorable.

Felicia did not hold the judge's hand. Maybe they weren't friends at that level. But just her presence there, steady by his side, was such a generous thing to offer. Maybe his bailiff was the only person Judge McCracken still had in his life who would sit with him in the hospital. Winnie admired Felicia for it. What a quality person.

And here was Winnie at home sipping lemon and honey tea, comfortable between her dogs.

She could do better.

Felicia was doing it right.

"Come on," Winnie told the dogs, rousting them from their comfort. "Let's go over to Auntie Dawn's. I'll be back in a while."

This time Winnie did not feel the need for a disguise. She dressed as herself, in comfortable dark blue fleece pants and an oversized blue flannel shirt and a purple fleece vest on top.

She was about to leave her house when she realized she needed something from her quilted gray purse. She tucked it into her vest pocket and headed for the hospital.

12

Felicia sat with her elbow propped on the metal chair arm and her chin resting in her hand. Winnie hated to wake her, but Felicia must have sensed someone come near. The instincts of a bailiff.

"Hello," Winnie said. "Remember me?"

Felicia nodded. And frowned. What was this old lady from court today doing at the judge's hospital bedside?

"How is he?" Winnie asked.

"Ma'am," Felicia said, "this isn't appropriate—"

Winnie pulled the three drawings out of her vest pocket and handed them to Felicia.

"My name is Dr. Winifred Parsons. I'm the plaintiffs' lawyer's aunt."

Felicia looked at her skeptically. "Uh-huh."

"I'm a retired professor," Winnie said. "I taught psychology at the U."

Felicia looked too tired for all this nonsense. But she flipped through the three drawings Winnie had given her. And Felicia seemed to recognize what she saw.

She gazed up at Winnie with new interest.

"I'm also clairvoyant," Winnie added.

Felicia sighed. "I'm listening."

Winnie found another metal chair and brought it next to Felicia's. The judge was still sleeping. He hadn't stirred since Winnie arrived.

"That's how I could see," Winnie said. "I knew he wasn't well. But I should have said something much earlier. I'm sorry I let it go so long. But you ... you got there in time. I'm so glad."

Felicia pressed a weary hand against her forehead. "Barely," she said. "I should have done something sooner, too. It's been getting worse for weeks."

"It's his retirement, isn't it?" Winnie asked. "And his wife, of course."

"We don't share much," Felicia said. "But yeah. I assume."

"But you know these drawings," Winnie said, pointing to them in Felicia's hands.

Felicia nodded. "I cleared them off his bench at lunchtime. I would have thought you stole them, but I shredded them myself. He always wants me to. So why are you here, exactly? What am I supposed to say?"

"It's what I want to say," Winnie answered. "You're a good person. I could see that the minute you walked into the courtroom today." Winnie gave her a warm smile. "Trust me, it's my talent." She grew serious again. "But Judge McCracken is hurting terribly. And I can see how it's endangering his life. I want to help, if I can. I lost my husband a few years ago, and I know the kind of pain he's been feeling. I thought I might talk to him, if you think that's all right."

Felicia glanced over at the sleeping judge.

"I don't know," she said. "He keeps things very personal."

"Why don't I wait here with the two of you for a while?" Winnie said. "We'll see how we feel about it. I don't need to be anywhere else."

They sat there in cramped quarters for another hour or so before someone came to wheel the judge into a private room of his own.

Felicia looked dead on her feet as she followed. But it wasn't Winnie's place to tell her to take a break or go home. This was a judge's bailiff. She had to be tough.

When the nurse came in to tend to his various tubes and wires, Winnie and Felicia went out to wait in the hall.

"You don't have to keep staying," Felicia said.

"You don't, either," Winnie answered. An image

flashed into her mind. "I can see your husband and two teenage girls waiting at home." Winnie paused a moment. "Twins?"

Felicia shook her head in amazement. "Okay, I believe you." She slouched against the nearby wall. "I'll go once he wakes up. I just want him to know I was here."

Winnie closed her eyes. Took a long breath. Felt her way forward into the night.

"He'll open his eyes at 10:43. He won't be awake long."

For the first time since Winnie arrived, Felicia seemed to brighten. A faint tinge of coral returned to her aura. Up until then it looked like layers of beige and dark brown. Winnie was glad to see the change.

Felicia glanced at the clock above them. It was already 10:07. "Okay," she said, pushing upright away from the wall. "I can wait that long."

Winnie thought about saying, "So can I," but she realized she had done all she could for the night. Judge McCracken wouldn't be up to talking to anyone for a while. Winnie might as well go home to bed.

But she could feel the shift in Felicia. That was what time and presence had done. Winnie knew it was right to ask now. Felicia was ready to accept.

"I'll come back tomorrow," Winnie said. "Later in the morning. Will you put in a good word for me with your judge? Show him the drawings. Tell him I saw what was making him sick. Tell him I want to help him with what I know."

Felicia looked Winnie directly in the eyes. As if assessing one last time whether this nice old lady could be trusted.

"Can I be here with him?" Felicia asked.

"That's fine with me," Winnie said. "Although what we talk about might be too personal for him."

"Too bad," Felicia said, suppressing a mighty yawn. "I know more than he thinks. And I'll know if he needs to listen to you."

That seemed fair enough. The two of them exchanged phone numbers so that Felicia could text her when the judge was ready for a visit the next day.

"Will you show him my drawings?" Winnie asked. "So he knows what to expect?"

"Depends on his mood," Felicia said. "But I'll at least tell him you're coming. After that it's up to you. I'm not going to try to convince him of anything."

Winnie patted her arm and left Felicia to wait the remaining half hour for Judge McCracken to wake up, see his bailiff sitting faithfully by his hospital bed, and smile in gratitude at her loyalty and kindness.

Winnie had already watched that scene in her mind's eye. She didn't need to see it again.

She made her weary way out to the parking lot. Other

people were coming and going at that time of night: doctors, nurses, family members, and friends. A hospital parking lot was never empty.

It was too late to pick up the dogs, so Winnie would have to sleep without them for a night. But she barely noticed once her head hit the pillow. She was out before Felicia would have even started for home.

In the morning Winnie resumed her familiar routine. She drank her coffee and meditated in bed, then wrote up six pages of notes from the day before.

She retrieved the dogs, bundled King Arthur into his little jacket, and took both of them on their respective walks: King Arthur on a short stroll around the neighborhood, then Clover on her longer circuit around the nearby university campus.

As she walked, breathing in the crisp morning air and savoring the golden winter sunshine on her face, Winnie thought about what she was going to say to the judge. How she could help him. What was the right way to approach him.

She knew there was still a risk that a serious, impressive person like him wouldn't believe her.

But she wouldn't let that stop her from telling him what she could.

Not this time. She had learned her lesson yesterday. No more holding back. Not when a man's survival could depend on it.

Still ... what exactly was she supposed to say?

And then, as it so often did, the answer popped into her mind like toast out of a toaster.

13

Judge McCracken sat up in bed wearing a hospital gown that made him look far from distinguished. In fact, he looked sadly diminished. His white hair stuck out at wispy angles, white stubble covered his chin and cheeks, and without his black robe over a white button-down shirt and blue-striped tie, he might pass as any old man you saw shuffling down the street.

On the brighter side, his aura was back to its familiar pale blue. No needles or skewers anywhere. And Winnie could see that some of the tears in his aura had mended themselves over night. Maybe being cared for in a medical setting had made his auric body feel safe. Winnie had seen so many different reactions over the years to people having to be hospitalized. Some of them immediately thrived, from their minds to their bodies to their souls.

Others rapidly declined. She couldn't sense at the moment which way Judge McCracken would go. She hoped for nothing but improvement.

Felicia was nowhere to be seen. Maybe she had stepped out to use the restroom or visit the cafeteria. But Winnie wouldn't wait for her. In fact, maybe it was better she wasn't there. Winnie had some very personal things to say to the judge.

She had already spent her quiet time this morning adjusting her mind. William McCracken was just a person. A widower. Soon to be retired, like she was. No one to be intimidated by, no matter how gruff he might get.

And thanks to her flash of insight while on her walk with Clover, she knew exactly how she was going to approach the matter.

Like a lawyer.

She imagined how Rose would do it. Straight forward. No hedging or hiding. Just speak plainly and make her case.

"Good morning," Winnie said. She resisted calling him *your honor*. She also refrained from holding out her hand to shake. That didn't seem wise in a hospital.

The judge did not respond. He simply looked at her. Winnie couldn't tell if he remembered her or recognized her from the day before. She was dressed as herself again, in long johns under loose khaki pants, a teal fleece sweater, and her gray overcoat. She carried a tan tote bag with a local library logo on it. The tote held a very important collection of papers.

A visitor's chair took up space between the bed and the window, but Winnie felt it was too forward of her to sit down. She thought about how she would react if a relative stranger came to visit her in the hospital and sat so close to her. She might feel trapped. That wasn't a good way to start.

Instead she stood at the nearer side of Judge McCracken's bed, out of the way of the metal pole holding his IV drip, and launched into her opening statement.

"I am Dr. Winifred Parsons. I have a Doctorate in Psychology and spent almost forty years teaching Consumer Psychology at the University of Arizona. I have multiple certifications and commendations. I am now retired."

She decided to leave out any mention of being Rose's aunt. She had revealed that to Felicia, but there was no point in repeating it directly to the judge, just in case. The trial still wasn't finished, and Winnie had no desire to get Rose into trouble. Better to leave that fact out.

Now came the more interesting part.

"In addition to my respected career as a professor," Winnie continued, "I am also a respected clairvoyant. That means that I see things and know things that most people do not. Yesterday I watched the condition of your body—"

She decided to call it his body, rather than his aura. He might not agree he had an aura, but he certainly couldn't deny he had a body.

"—deteriorate over the course of the day until I realized you were in danger of collapsing. Your bailiff can verify that I was the one who shouted for someone to catch you just a moment before you fell from the bench—"

"I can," came a voice behind them. "You probably didn't hear her," Felicia said as she continued toward them and took up her spot in the visitor's chair, "but this lady was the one."

Felicia pried open the lid of the coffee cup she'd brought back. Steam rose from the center. She motioned for Winnie to continue.

But that was the extent of Winnie's opening speech. She had practiced it several times on her drive to the hospital until she felt comfortable that it stated the relevant facts while also identifying her true abilities. She would not apologize for what she could see and do. She was proud of it. She wanted to help Judge McCracken with every ounce of her gift.

Now Winnie reverted to professor mode. "Do you have any questions so far?" She always wanted clarity when she taught her students. Right now, Judge William

McCracken was her newest student.

The judge said nothing. He showed no expression, either way. Not skeptical, not accepting, nothing. Felicia calmly sipped her coffee and watched.

"Then on we go," Winnie said.

She knew that this time *she* was the show. She had better keep her audience engaged. She saw what happened whenever Judge McCracken's attention started to wander. And if Felicia was staying for this deeply personal part, Winnie had to be careful how she played it.

She reached into the tote bag and pulled out a yellow folder. In it were several loose-leaf sheets of notebook paper. Winnie kept the handle of the tote draped over her elbow as she opened the folder and prepared to read. But part of a bailiff's job was to maintain order in the courtroom, and Felicia obviously felt Winnie was lacking order.

"Here, sit down," Felicia said, relinquishing her chair. "I'll get another."

"I'm all ri—"

"*Sit*," Felicia ordered.

Finally Judge McCracken spoke. "Best not to argue."

Winnie shot him a conspiratorial smile as she moved into Felicia's chair. The bailiff carried in another from the hallway and set it up at the foot of the judge's bed.

"There," Felicia said. "Now go. Tell him about these drawings."

Winnie knew an ally when she found one. She closed

her folder and accepted the three pieces of paper from Felicia.

"I tuned my hand into yours," Winnie said. "That's the best way I can explain it. I drew most of this with my eyes closed."

Judge McCracken held out his hand for the pictures. Winnie noticed his hand trembled a little. The judge took his time inspecting the drawings. Winnie waited in silence.

At last he asked her, "Do you know where this is?"

Winnie was about to automatically answer no, assuming he wanted to tell her about it himself, but then she realized this was a test.

"Wait," she said. She closed her eyes and turned on her flashlight in the warehouse.

"Ogunquit, Maine," she said. "September eighteenth, six years ago. I see you sitting on a rocky shore, drawing in a sketchbook. You're wearing black rain pants and a blue raincoat. Dark clouds are moving in, but it hasn't rained yet. Helen is with you. She laughed when you said you wanted to come out here now. She said you'd both get soaked. But you wanted to try to capture the way the waves looked as they crashed against the rocks under a stormy sky. You always love to draw the ocean."

Winnie opened her eyes. The judge was staring at her with a look of both pain and wonder.

His voice came out soft and hoarse. "What is Helen doing?"

Winnie closed her eyes again. Returned to the scene in her mind. "She's wearing rain gear, too. Black pants and a yellow raincoat. She has her hair back in a ponytail. It's a beautiful silver color. She's wearing a black baseball cap with yellow lettering. It says..." Winnie had to shift her vision to look closer. "Maud's Beach."

She heard the judge's breath catch.

But Winnie stayed with Helen. "She took off her shoes and rolled up her pants, and now she's out wading at the edge of the water. She likes to dig her bare toes into the sand. She ... hurt her left foot when she was young. Something about a bike?"

"Caught her foot in the spokes," Judge McCracken confirmed. "When she was six."

"And walking barefoot in the sand feels as good as—"

"Someone massaging it," Judge McCracken said with Winnie.

Winnie opened her eyes. She met the judge's gaze. "Do you want me to go on?"

"Yes," he said, "for the next ten hours. It's all I want to hear."

Winnie could see the change in his aura. For the first time since she began observing him yesterday, a light green band now encircled his chest. And up near his right temple, small dots of lilac floated at the edge of his outline.

Lilac was good. Green was generally good. Winnie felt encouraged.

"No offense, sir," Felicia broke in to say, "but if this is what you two are talking about all day, I have some paperwork back at court I need to look after."

Felicia held out her hand toward Winnie. "So can I leave her with you? Everything okay?"

The judge nodded.

"Need anything?" Felicia asked him. "Water, the nurse, anything?"

"No, Felicia. Thank you." The judge cleared his throat and said it again. "Thank you. For everything."

Felicia gave him a short nod, then pushed out of her chair. For the first time Winnie noticed how she was dressed, in another pant suit, just like yesterday. Winnie forgot this was another work day. Retirement meant all of her own days were generally the same. But she imagined a bailiff still had plenty to do, even if her judge was laid up in the hospital.

As she passed behind Winnie, Felicia gave her shoulder a quick squeeze. "Don't you upset him," Felicia said. "Or I'll hear about it."

Then she left Winnie and the judge alone.

The judge cleared his throat again. Let out a brief cough. Then he gestured toward where Winnie last saw several skewers piercing his neck. "They tell me there's a node in there, on my thyroid gland. Not my imagination. I actually do have a lump in my throat."

He said it without smiling. This was no joke. Winnie remembered the way her own throat seemed to close in the first months after Joe died. She swallowed so many tears, some days it seemed there was no room for food. She thought she might choke on even water.

Winnie knew it was time. The judge had volunteered something personal about himself. The opening was there.

But she still had to approach him gently. She could feel how the wound was still raw and tender.

"I need to tell you about something else I saw," Winnie said. "Something about Helen."

The green band around the judge's chest expanded and contracted. As if his aura took a deep and bracing breath all on its own. Winnie took that as a good sign. And the fact that the band was still bright green was also good. It meant so far he hadn't shut down.

"Go ahead," Judge McCracken told her. His voice sounded strained, but Winnie saw a hopeful look in his eyes.

She knew what it was like to hear stories about Joe after he died. Winnie was hungry for every single memory someone wanted to share. It was like looking at pictures of him. Reading all the cards she saved that he had given her over the years. All of them tangible traces of the man she had loved and the life she loved living with him.

But this story would be different. The memory would likely hurt. But Winnie needed to start there to get to the other side.

She reached into her tote and pulled out the yellow file.

"It's about the night she died," Winnie said quietly. "Are you ready?"

14

The judge had had a contentious day in court. The opposing attorneys took snipes at each other, at each others' clients, at the mediator who had failed to wrestle a settlement out of everyone a few days prior, and it was generally everyone else's fault.

Bill McCracken missed the old days when lawyers still had some manners. He missed the formalities that reminded everyone this was a court of law, they were officers of the court, and everyone had better act like they understood this was a noble and important profession.

But these days all the formalities looked old-fashioned and pointless. Everything was fast, so fast, and had to be digital and slick and above all else, entertaining.

The law was not meant to be entertainment. It was

meant to keep the scales balanced, always seeking out the good and the right and the true.

Sometimes Bill had to treat the lawyers like children. Scold them, even yell at them, wrangle them like preschoolers.

If that made him unpopular, so be it. If they called him old, grouchy, out of touch behind his back, then fine. What part of that wasn't true? Judge William McCracken was old school, and he wasn't going to change just because newer judges were coming onto the bench and had their own ideas of how their courts should be run.

Bill appreciated his staff. Felicia had been with him for almost twenty years now. She understood how he liked things to be.

He'd had a few different court clerks over the decades, but this one, Alyssa, had stuck around almost ten. She had the right attitude about organization and paperwork and generally How Things Should Be.

They were an efficient little unit, Judge McCracken's courtroom. It took a lot of years to get it to run as smoothly as he liked, but most days he felt they had done it. Even today, when the bickering lawyers had been so exhausting.

He left the courthouse a little before five. He liked to beat the downtown traffic. It was a Tuesday, and that meant Helen had visited her sister that morning. Bill wondered what the latest drama would be.

But not the two of them. "We have no problems," Helen said every time she told a story of her sister's latest disasters or some friend who hated her husband, or anyone having any kind of strife in their life. "We have no problems."

"Good," Bill would say back. "Let's keep it that way."

Helen was in their bedroom sorting out clothes to take to the ladies' charity down the street. Part of her spring cleaning. She kept a neat and tidy house.

Bill tried to do his part, hanging up his jacket, putting his shirt in the hamper, mindful of not leaving his day's work clothes just strewn all over the house.

"How was it?" Helen asked him when he found her in the bedroom.

"Nee-nee-nee," he imitated the squabbling lawyers. "No fair, I had it first."

Helen chuckled. "I'm sure you set them right."

Bill toed the back of his polished leather shoes and put them in their proper place in the closet. He hung up his tie—no salsa stains from lunch this time, so he could safely wear it again. Helen was always a stickler for that. *"You're a judge. Show some pride."*

He changed into Gramicci shorts and an old T-shirt he bought years ago in Alaska.

"Subtle," Helen said, noticing it.

"Did you find something yet?" Bill asked.

"Been run off my feet today. I'll look at it tonight."

Bill had blocked off two weeks of his court calendar at the end of May. It would still be cold the places where they wanted to go, but this way they could beat the summer crowds.

"Should we go someplace new or someplace old?" Helen asked him when they first starting planning a few weeks ago.

"Your choice," Bill said. "Just get me away."

The location might still be a mystery at this point, but the kind of place was not: Water. Always water. Somewhere where they could look out over the ocean, stroll on a beach, listen to waves rolling night and day.

Bill loved to sketch it. Sometimes he'd even bring out his traveling watercolor kit and brush the scenery in color onto the page. But mostly he just loved sitting with pencil and pad and capturing the beauty one line and curve at a time.

Helen had her own love affair with the ocean. She could sit for hours just looking out over the water and studying the sky and the birds and the waves.

"You're never bored?" he asked her once after he'd spent over two hours immersed in his sketching.

"How could I be?" Helen answered, sweeping her arm over the landscape. "Look at it."

They had tried sea kayaking in New Zealand. Whale watching in Alaska. Cruises that lasted days or weeks. On one trip they paid a ridiculous amount of money to swim with dolphins. One of the best experiences of their lives.

How they both ended up living in the desert south-west, meeting and falling in love when they were students at the University of Arizona, sticking around to pursue their professions instead of escaping to someplace near the sea was still a mystery to them both. "One thing led to another," Helen told people who asked her the same thing. That seemed like the story of their life. One thing led to another.

And for almost fifty years, that story was wonderful. Unmatchable. The best.

And now it was all over. Suddenly and tragically. William McCracken's best friend and love his life was gone in the blink of an eye. In the unbeating of a heartbeat.

"You know what she was reading," Winnie said. "I'm sure you looked at it."

Judge McCracken nodded. He swallowed past the node in his throat. Gathered himself, made sure he could say it without emotion. "Alaska tours."

"The book fell to the ground when she dropped it," Winnie said. "So you don't know what page she saw. Why she laughed. You heard her laugh, didn't you?"

Now Judge McCracken couldn't stop the flow of tears. He pressed his lips together and nodded.

"It's why..." He paused. Cleared his throat. He used the

sleeve of his hospital gown to swipe his face dry. "It's why I first noticed her. That laugh. Beautiful."

Winnie took over from here. She didn't need to force him to talk. She remembered too well how hard it was sometimes. The pain of it, trying to shape her feelings into words.

"She was flipping through the Alaskan tour book," Winnie said. "She found a whale-watching tour in Ketchikan. You two went on it before, many years ago."

"I remember," the judge whispered.

"Do you remember the joke?" Winnie asked. She had heard it in Helen McCracken's head at the same moment she heard Helen's beautiful laugh.

Judge McCracken seemed puzzled for a moment. But then yes, he nodded. "How do you know?" he asked Winnie. "How could you possibly know?"

"Tell me if I get it right," she said, although she was fairly certain she would. "The tour operator was young. Maybe early thirties. Very enthusiastic about his job."

"Very," the judge agreed. Winnie could see the beginning of a wistful smile.

"He was an amateur magician, too," Winnie said, although that fact seemed wrong when she first saw it. But her mini-movies didn't lie, even though they often surprised her.

Again the judge nodded. "Crap at it, if you want the truth."

"But that was what made it fun," Winnie said. "The passengers liked him all the more because he was so awkward."

"True," Judge McCracken said. "What was his name?" It didn't sound like he was testing her this time. He honestly wanted to remember.

"Davy."

"Davy," the judge repeated. "From the navy."

Winnie smiled. "It was a good schtick. Davy kept talking and talking, telling you all a hundred facts about whales and whale pods and whale family units and whale song…"

"Wouldn't shut up," the judge confirmed.

"But he knew his stuff," Winnie said.

"That he did."

"He took you right to where you could see them."

The judge nodded. Winnie went on. She described the whole scene of a family of whales—six of them—breaching the water right in front of the boat.

"And then Davy said…" She waited for the judge. He remembered. She knew he did.

"*Don't worry if you see a whale's tail,*" he recited. "*It's just a fluke.*"

Winnie met the judge's gaze. "Terrible joke."

"Then he made it worse by trying to explain it. 'Get it? A whale's tail is called a fluke.' Kid should have stopped at the punchline."

"But it is kind of funny," Winnie admitted.

"Helen sure thought so," the judge said. "She had a sweatshirt made for me that said the same thing. She thought it was ridiculously clever."

"She found the same tour," Winnie said softly. "She was going to suggest you take it. Did you know that?"

Judge McCracken shook his head. Winnie could see the information taking hold. She wondered how it made him feel.

"That was why she laughed," the judge said.

"Yes. She was just about to tell you."

The judge's eyes moistened again. He swiped back of his hand over his right eye. He sighed and let out a soft curse.

Winnie sat quietly for the next few minutes. This was not a time for filling the air with words.

She could see that moment in her mind's eye: Helen finding the tour. Her laugh of delight...

The judge's voice broke the silence. "Can you tell me why?"

Winnie expected the question. It was a natural thing to ask. Especially to ask someone like Winnie with her access to special knowledge.

She shook her head. "I'm sorry. I can't. If you mean why ... in an overall sense. It doesn't make sense. It won't."

The judge looked at her, maybe assessing the truth of that statement for himself.

"I've gone around and around it," he said.

"I know," Winnie answered. "But it doesn't actually help. It only keeps freshening the wound."

The judge gave her a piercing look. As if she were a witness on the stand, trying to get away with not telling the truth, the whole truth, and nothing but the truth.

"How do you know that?" he demanded.

"Because I did it, too."

Winnie could see how her answer caught him off guard. Good. She needed him to listen.

"You lost somebody?" he asked. And Winnie saw the band of green around his chest grow thinner and tighter than before.

But it was also true that his overall aura was now a deeper shade of blue, with fewer rips in it, fewer places where his energy was leaking out.

Talking about this out loud—maybe for the first time in the past year—seemed to be doing the judge some good. Winnie needed to keep going.

"My husband Joe," she said. "Not suddenly like Helen, but still too soon."

Judge McCracken looked down at his hands. Winnie could see the veins of years on the backs of them, maybe even more pronounced because they were the hands of an artist. "I'm ... I'm sorry." His voice sounded thick. Then the tears began to flow again. The judge lifted his right hand

and pinched his fingers against his eyes. "Sometimes it feels like all I do is cry."

"You won't forever," Winnie said. "But I still do sometimes. It's been three years, and it's not all day anymore, not even every day or week. But all it takes is some thought or memory or someone saying something about him..." She pretended to scratch at her left forearm. "I find it's always right there, just under the hairs of my arm."

"So it will never go away," the judge said.

"Why should it?" Winnie asked. She could feel heat rising on her cheeks. She hardly ever said this out loud, but she thought it all the time. "I loved him. You loved Helen. We don't need to pretend it's fine. It's not fine. We don't agree with it. We'll never agree with it. We have to put up with it, but we're never going to say it's all right."

The judge gazed at her in astonishment. As if what she was saying was so radical, no one in polite company would dare say it. "But then ... how? How are you supposed to go on?"

"That was exactly what I kept asking Joe," Winnie said. "Those last few days of his life. He was thin and dying and in pain. When he finally slipped into a coma, I was so relieved for him.

"But not relieved for me. I knew it was almost over. And even though I wouldn't make him stay an hour longer when he was in so much pain, I still hated that he was leaving.

"*How am I supposed to go on?*

"And then the night before he died, he sent me a vision. It wasn't a dream. I wasn't sleeping. I was awake. I was lying on our bed next to him. I didn't want to leave his side, in case he ever woke up. I wanted him to know I was there."

The door to the judge's hospital room opened just then and a nurse came striding in. "Hi! How nice, you have a visitor! I just need to check your fluids. How are you feeling?"

"Fine," the judge snapped. It was clear he wasn't in the mood for chitchat. But he did take a moment to push himself up against his pillows. He sat up straighter. Winnie could see the dignified judge after all. He didn't want to look sickly or weak. Even with his unkempt hair and unshaven face and shapeless, faded hospital gown, he still wanted to present himself properly to the world.

The nurse pulled on a pair of purple disposable gloves and began fiddling with bags hanging from the IV pole.

By unspoken agreement Winnie and the judge both waited in silence. Their conversation was not one to continue in front of a stranger.

When the nurse finished her work, Winnie waited for the door to close behind her before continuing.

"A vision," the judge prompted.

"Yes. I saw Joe standing in front of me, at the side of the bed. He looked wonderful. Healthy and strong. Filled out again. Not so thin he looked like a skeleton. His face had color again. He was the Joe from a year ago, before he ever got sick."

"I would give anything to see Helen again," the judge said. "Even for a minute."

"I know," Winnie said. "Believe me. Seeing Joe that one last time was an absolute gift. I was so grateful for it then and I still am. And what he said to me ... did it make it all right that he was dying? No. But I knew what he said was true. And it has helped me. I think it might help you, too."

Winnie checked the judge's aura: a dark, sky blue, thick all around. The green band encircling his chest had widened again. Despite the intensity of their conversation, it looked as if the judge might actually feel relaxed. The lilac dots floating around his temple brought a softness to the area where Winnie had seen so many needles bristling outward the day before.

Winnie ventured on.

"I didn't want to hear it," she said. "Let me be clear about that. I didn't want to hear Joe say it would be all right, I would find a way—none of it."

"You're a tough customer," the judge observed.

"Aren't you?" she replied. "If Helen had said, 'Oh, Bill,

you'll be fine. You'll get over it'—do you think you would have appreciated that?"

"Hell no."

"Hell no," Winnie agreed. "And Joe didn't try any of that. He knew me perfectly well.

"And one of the things he knows about me is that I love to learn. I can't stop myself. I'm curious about so many things. All the time. I bet you're the same way."

The judge nodded. He was listening.

"So that's how he got me," Winnie said. She closed her eyes. Brought the scene back into her mind. How many times had she already watched it? Fifty. A hundred. More. It didn't matter. She would watch it as many times as she wanted.

Joe standing beside their bed. Gazing down at her with such love in his eyes. Winnie tried to sit up, to embrace him, to touch him, but her body stayed locked to the bed.

"He told me, 'I had my life. You still have yours. You're still so curious about so many things. So use the rest of your time to find out everything you still want to know. About everything. Ask yourself every day: What do I wonder about? Then go find out.'"

"Hm," Judge McCracken mumbled. He took it in for a moment. Winnie could feel him weighing it in his mind. "So, did it help?"

"Not in the beginning," she said. "Not for a while. I still missed him every single day. I still grieved. But I did keep that question in mind. Even though some days the only thing I wondered about was whether I would ever feel happy again."

"Because being happy feels ... obscene," the judge said.

"It does," Winnie agreed. "That's definitely part of it. You understand."

"Not that I've had many moments of happiness this past year..." the judge said.

"But sometimes they sneak up on you," Winnie said. "You're doing something you enjoy, and then you catch yourself. As if for a minute you forgot what matters."

The judge nodded. "Sometimes when I'm drawing."

Ah. That explained what Winnie observed the day before. When the judge was quiet and sketching, suddenly the needles and skewers showed up. The only way to fight them was to become aggressive.

While he drew, he felt peace. Satisfaction. Maybe even the beginning of happiness.

But he wasn't ready to be happy. How could he be, when Helen was gone?

Logical or not, Winnie understood that perfectly. But she refrained from telling the judge about his aura and the needles. He had adjusted well enough to so much new information, but Winnie didn't want to lose him by going too far.

"So ... did it ever get better?" the judge asked.

"Slowly," Winnie said. "Over time. But it did take time. It was nothing I could push or force. I didn't want to. That didn't seem kind to myself.

"But yes, eventually I did feel things begin to change. I started wondering, just like Joe said. And one of the things I wondered—because I'd already been wondering it for a long time before then—was whether I really could help people with my gift. I had been so careful my whole life and I wanted very few people to know. But there were times when I thought if I were just brave enough I could really make a difference in some people's lives.

"And so I started trying," Winnie said. "I helped one person, that felt good, so I helped another. And people were very grateful. I was still cautious about it—I still am. I don't announce it from the rooftops—and I treat my gift seriously. I charge people for my time, just like a doctor or lawyer—mostly so they take me seriously, too."

"Makes sense," the judge said. "A five-hundred-dollar an hour lawyer has to be a lot better than a two-hundred an hour. Perception, whether it's true or not."

"You ask if it's gotten better," Winnie said. "Yes, it has. And also no, it never will. But that's how it is. This is reality. And I can either keep sitting in the dirt, or get up and keep walking."

"I've been doing a lot of that," the judge said. "Both.

Sitting in the dirt and then getting disgusted with myself and getting back up and walking."

"But you know what?" Winnie said. "One day I finally realized what I'd gotten wrong: Joe's death was about him, it wasn't about me. It wasn't some test for me. It certainly wasn't a punishment. It was Joe's life and it was how the whole life played out. It wasn't about me.

"Joe was right. He had his life and I still had mine. He didn't need me to suffer or stop living. Any of that was irrelevant to him anymore. He didn't need me. Helen doesn't need you."

She watched for the judge's reaction to that. He didn't seem to like what she was saying, but he could take it. His aura looked fine. Winnie even thought the lines on his face looked a little less deep, as though a layer of pain had relaxed.

"I still love my husband," she said. "I will always love him. I know he loved me and still does, at some level I don't fully understand because I don't live there.

"You will always love Helen, but her death wasn't about you. That was her life. You still have yours."

Winnie could feel it: she was reaching the end of her case. This was now her closing argument. It would be up to the judge to decide what was right. All Winnie could do was present all the facts.

"You and I both suffered the loss of our favorite people," she said. "That happened to us. We can't undo it.

But now we still have these lives of our own and what we do with them is what our lives still are.

"And so I think that's what you have to decide now, for yourself. How do you want your life to be now that it's not the way you preferred? You're on your own. You have to retire. So what do you do next? What are you still curious to know?

"I think if you're honest you know the answer to that. If I asked you to pick just one thing you want to know about next, I bet you could tell me right now.

"So go on," Winnie challenged him. "Tell me."

She sat back and folded her hands in her lap.

The judge was silent for a moment, considering. "You're serious?"

"I am," Winnie said. "Pick one thing. Right now."

She surprised herself with her boldness. Since when did she feel she had the right to boss around a trial court judge? But this was no time to back down. She needed to press her advantage. Her case wasn't over yet. The judge hadn't rendered his verdict.

"I'm curious about waves," he said.

"All right."

"How to draw them."

"Okay."

"There's a ... class," the judge said. "In Maine. It's with a teacher I took a class from before. It's that day you saw me on the beach with Helen."

"Good," Winnie said. "When is it?"

"Every September."

"That's a long way off," Winnie said. "But you can sign up for it now, and still do something in between. So what else are you curious about?"

The judge shifted uncomfortably in his bed. She was making him nervous. Winnie didn't mind.

Sometimes it was the only way to move people forward from where they were. She was here to help. It looked like she was.

"There's that trip. The one in Alaska. The one you said Helen was looking at. Whale watching in May."

"Wonderful. But be honest with yourself. Do you think it will make you too sad?"

Winnie asked it without the slightest hint of sympathy. It was just a practical question, like asking someone if they could walk yet on that broken leg.

"Probably," the judge said. "But you didn't ask me what sounded fun, you asked me what I'm curious about. And I'm always curious about whales."

Winnie was curious about something herself. She pointed to the drawings still gathered on the judge's lap.

"What was that one with the bracelet?" she asked. "What did that mean?"

"I bought it for Helen after that whale-watching tour. Paid a ridiculous amount for it. It was worth it. She wore it almost every day. I bought her plenty of other jewelry over the years, but somehow that one was always her favorite."

Winnie saw a flash of it now. She had missed it before.

"She was wearing it the night she died."

Judge McCracken nodded. "I keep it in my pocket." He glanced down at his hospital gown. "When I have pockets." He pointed to a cabinet across from the foot of his bed. "I don't mind you looking."

Winnie got up and opened the tall, thin cabinet. The judge's shoes sat at the bottom and his clothing from yesterday hung on hooks. Winnie felt self-conscious rooting around in Judge McCracken's trouser pockets, but she found the bracelet quickly and pulled it out.

The braided strip was made of smooth navy blue cord. It reminded Winnie of craft projects she made when she was young. But the clasp was special: a fluke made of sterling silver.

"I had it engraved," the judge said. "You can read it."

"*Our love is no fluke*," Winnie read out loud. She tilted her head. "Really? And you're making fun of the tour guide?"

For the first time, the judge genuinely smiled. He also looked slightly embarrassed. But Winnie told him truthfully, "That's very sweet."

He shrugged. "Helen thought so. That's all that mattered." He reached out his hand for the bracelet.

Winnie placed it in his palm. The judge ran his thumb over the smooth silver fluke.

"Every day," he muttered.

"Every day," Winnie said. "But they deserve it, don't they? Helen and Joe still deserve our love."

Judge McCracken closed the bracelet in his fist. He gazed at Winnie and sighed.

"So that's it," he said.

"Your honor, I rest my case."

The judge seemed tired. But his aura looked strong. Stronger than Winnie had seen it before. The blue outline looked thick and whole. The green band around his chest breathed in and out freely. The lilac dots around his temple looked plump like blueberries.

Winnie could honestly say she was leaving him better than she found him. And that was exactly what she hoped.

The judge's gaze met Winnie's. "I'm going to think about everything you said. It's ... hard, but I think I see what you mean." He bowed his head in a respectful nod. "Dr. Parsons, I thank you."

"Judge McCracken, it was my pleasure."

Out in the late morning sunshine, Winnie paused on the way to her car.

Had she done enough? Said enough? Had she really made any difference?

Judge McCracken's life wasn't her life. Just as her life

wasn't Joe's. Each of them—everyone—had their own individual path. All Winnie could do was do her best.

Then be satisfied and move on.

She picked up the dogs from Auntie Dawn's. "They probably think they live here by now."

"Fine with me," Dawn said. "Sporty had a blast. They actually play with him. They're not just on the computer all day. So Sporty's vote is, more."

But Winnie was ready to return to her routines. Walks, baking, reading, sitting on the couch between the dogs under a blanket—all of the cozy elements.

She called Rose that evening, after she was sure they were done with their supper. Winnie had her news, but Rose had hers, too.

"Ha. Beasley quit. He filed his Motion to Withdraw this afternoon."

"So what does that mean?" Winnie asked. "For the case?"

"Barr is going to have to find someone else to represent him in time for a new trial. We're still assigned to McCracken, even though word is he won't be done with his surgery and recovery for at least the next month."

"Doesn't he have to retire soon after that?" Winnie asked.

"He does. But we got the notice that we're still on his trial calendar right before then, so I guess he wants to see it through."

Winnie was about to ask more about it, but Rose cut her off. "That's not the best thing," she said. "I found Sabrina Rich a lawyer to take her case in San Diego. They're going to file a fraud claim there, too. And I bet there are other people Barr cheated. Maybe ... my law firm can hire you to help me find out?"

"I have to think about it," Winnie said. But her heart was already telling her no. It was one thing to help Rose with her case, and to help those nice people the Tudors, but Winnie didn't like the sound of being exposed to Rose's whole law firm. Winnie still valued her privacy. She wanted to be the one to decide on a case-by-case basis which people she helped and which ones could know about her gift.

The Tudors had no reason to suspect the part Winnie played, and she wanted it to stay that way.

"If something comes to me, I'll tell you," Winnie promised. Maybe some morning when she was sipping her coffee and snuggled up between the dogs, another singer-songwriter's name would pop into her head. It could happen. Then Winnie would gladly share her knowledge.

"One more thing," Rose said. "I know you don't like to go out at night..."

"Generally, no." Winnie loved her quiet nights of dogs and TV and reading. But occasionally she made an exception.

"Jennie and Mike invited us—they specifically said, bring your aunt. They're playing Friday night at the Desert Oasis Hotel. Can I tempt you?"

Winnie saw a flash again: of Jennie Tudor in her sparkly outfit, her long brown hair curling down her back. Of Mike Tudor wearing black jeans and black boots and a dark gray shirt. Jennie on keyboard, Mike sitting on a stool beside her playing guitar. The two of them smiling with joy as they sang one of Jennie's gorgeous love songs to each other.

Yes, Winnie would leave the house for that.

And if it went past her regular bedtime, then Sporty could enjoy a sleepover with Clover and King Arthur on a Friday night.

"Okay, it's a date."

15

Victor Barr had a new lawyer. But by the time the trial was scheduled to resume, the case had already settled.

Rose called Winnie with the news.

"We've nullified the contracts," Rose said. "All rights returned to Jennie and Mike—and Sabrina Rich. And Garson Mose. Thanks to you."

Garson Mose was a name that popped into Winnie's mind one day as she trimmed back the dead leaves on her bougainvillea. He lived in Nashville, Tennessee. He had been working in a diner for the past two years after losing his entire music catalog to that thief Victor Barr.

Winnie saw the whole, predictable fraud unfold in a mini-movie playing in her mind. She wrote down as many details as she could remember, then sent all the information to Rose.

Garson filed his own lawsuit in Tennessee. Rose said it would probably take another two years before that case went to trial.

But then Rose and the other lawyers formed a united front and came after Vic Barr with everything they had.

Winnie plugged her headset into the phone so she freed up her hands to pull a sheet of peanut butter and chocolate chip cookies out of the oven. She woke up that morning in the mood for them. And they were her neighbor Dawn's favorites. Winnie would take some over to her later.

She set the cookie sheet on the stove to cool and went into the living room to sit down. Clover had her chin on the cushioned arm of the couch. King Arthur slept curled up beside her. They had both already enjoyed their long morning walks. Winnie had the rest of the day to herself to make cookies, organize her bookshelves, and catch up on some of the psychology journals that had been stacking up in her to-read pile.

"What about the money?" Winnie asked.

"We compromised," Rose said. "We didn't get it all, but we got most of it. Jennie and Mike were fine with it. They just wanted it all to be over."

"So Barr still got away with some of it." That didn't sit

right with Winnie, but she knew that life wasn't always fair.

"Mm ... not really," Rose said.

Winnie could hear a certain sly tone in Rose's voice. A secret she hadn't yet told.

"Turns out one of the songs Barr took from Garson Mose is a huge hit over in Germany. They play it almost every week on some series everyone's watching. I don't know how it all came about, but apparently the music producer on the show needed a couple of love songs, and that's not really Garson's thing. He's more of a our-love-is-gone kind of guy, not an I'll-love-you-forever."

Winnie's skin tingled. She had a suspicion what Rose was about to say, but she wanted to hear the actual words. Already her heart was beating faster in anticipation.

"So one thing led to another..." Rose said.

"Jennie Tudor."

"That's right," Rose said, the pleasure coming through clearly in her voice. "And what I know and you know is that if you hadn't found Garson Mose for us, none of that would have happened. So in a way..."

"The slimeball almost did Jennie Tudor a favor."

"Almost," Rose agreed. "Let's not get carried away."

Winnie got up from the couch. The cookies were cool enough to enjoy with a cup of coffee. She needed the celebration. This was all so unexpectedly wonderful.

"Aunt Winnie, did you know when I came over that

night last month so upset about Judge McCracken that you'd end up helping so many people?"

Winnie had gotten a text from the judge just last week. Felicia must have given him Winnie's number.

Going to see whales in May in Alaska. Thank you again. I mean it.

"I didn't know," Winnie said. "But it makes me very glad to hear it."

Because people what they did for a reason. *La raison sage*. The wise reason. There must be some benefit. Some payoff. Whether people understood it in the moment or not.

For Winnie, it was the feeling she had right now, standing at her kitchen counter, sinking her teeth into a delicious cookie, listening to her niece tell her so much good news. It was the feeling of coziness and comfort that came from living in the same house where she had spent so many happy years with Joe. It was the love she felt for her family, her friends, and her dogs. It was the pride she took in her abilities.

And it was the satisfaction she felt every time she used those abilities to help someone else in the world. She felt that now: the warmth in her heart, along with the keen pleasure in her mind from having pursued just the latest in an endless list of all the things she was still curious about and wanted to know.

This was her life now. And it was a good life. Even if it wasn't the life she preferred to have. Just as the judge would have preferred going whale-watching with his beloved Helen by his side.

There were still whales in the world. And waves. And an ocean Judge McCracken could sketch for hours and hours. He still needed to know more—and so did Winnie. So much more, every single day.

Spending a life finding out was a very good life. Winnie was *making* it a very good life.

And now she was ready to find out what was next.

The mind is a mysterious place. And the truth can change your life.

5 Winnie Parsons Mystery Stories

Stories of life after death, miracle healings, communication with other species, and more.

Open up your heart
to the love of a
good dog.

ABOUT THE AUTHOR

Robin Brande is an award-winning author, former trial attorney, black belt in martial arts, wilderness medic, and Reiki Master.

She writes in multiple genres, including mystery, fantasy, science fiction, young adult, romance, and self-help. She is also a designer and maker whose work celebrates the bookish life.

For more information:
robinbrande.com